PIANO KEYS

IT CAME UPON A MIDNIGHT CLEAR (A HOLIDAY NOVELLA)

CHINA

CONTENTS

ISBN: 9781513674964

Time flies over us but leaves its shadow behind.
-Nathaniel Hawthorne

PROLOGUE

CHRISTMAS EVE 1995

"Justice, your mom has a really bad headache, and your dad is going to take her to the Emergency Room down the street," Marilyn leaned in and whispered in her nephew's ear.

"Nooo! Auntie Lyn, she's gotta stay a little longer, I got a big surprise for her. Please don't let her go. Please!" Justice begged.

"Justice, are you ready? Your performance begins in 5 minutes. Report to the stage in 3 minutes. Hurry! Hurry!" Justice's manager: Cali Langley, anxiously informed him.

"Cali, calm down. He's ready, give him a minute," Marilyn shooed the overzealous manager away.

"Auntie Lyn, promise you'll make her stay for my ENTIRE performance. Promise me!" Justice stood his lanky 5'4 frame in front of his aunt and put his hands together like he was praying. "Promise me, pleeaassee!"

"Ok! Ok! Let me go talk to your mom! Don't worry, she will see your performance, I will make sure of it."

Marilyn hugged Justice tightly and kissed him on his forehead. "Break a leg, my little piano prodigy you! Love you, and we will see you after the performance." She left the backstage area to convince her sister to stay to hear Justice play.

"Carol, we gotta go. You're seeing spots. Your headache is too bad for you to stay any longer. Let's go NOW!" Paul tried to put his foot down with his wife, but he knew it was pointless. She would never miss their only child's first performance at the FedEx Forum.

"Paul Benoit, I don't know who you're talking to like that, but you know damn well I have NEVER missed any of J.B.'s performances... since he was 4, and God-willing, I never will."

Carolyn Benoit pressed her fingers against her temples to try to relieve her excruciatingly painful headache. She was also dizzy and struggling to maintain her balance. The pain was so unbearable, she had to close her eyes tightly to stop the tears from forming.

Her husband shook his head in anger because of his wife's stubbornness. He wanted to pick her up and throw her over his shoulders like a caveman to force her to go to the hospital, but he knew that would only stress her out more. Succumbing to defeat, Paul threw his hands up and helped his wife ease into their front row seats.

"Ludwig Van Beethoven, Johann Sebastian Bach, Frederic Chopin, Alice Coltrane, Count Basie, Alicia Keys, John Legend...," Carolyn whispered the names of every composer on Justice's playlist as his ten-year-old fingers effortlessly glided over the piano keys.

She smiled proudly at her son in his black tuxedo with the traditional tails that hung over the piano bench while battling the headache that felt like her brain was about to explode. Carolyn could no longer hold the tears back, so she let them fall silently.

Gripping Paul's arm to push the pain away, she knew it was time to go.

"Paul, please take me to the E.R. I can't take it any longer." Her hands trembled and her voice shook as she leaned into her husband for support to stand up.

Her identical twin sister: Marilyn, was seated nearby and saw Carolyn and Paul getting ready to leave. She remembered her promise to Justice and walked over to see what was happening.

"Paul, is she ok? Has the headache gotten worse?" She looked at her sister and knew the answer to her questions. Carolyn's light complexion was fiery red. If "fever" were a person, her sister would be the face. Marilyn knew her twin was sick and something inside of her told her that the headache was far worse than what her sister was telling them.

"I'm sorry Justice, I gotta break my promise. I agree with your dad, your mom must go now. She can't wait," Carolyn said to herself and started helping her brother-in-law with her sister.

Slowly, they made it up the aisle. Marilyn could barely hold herself up, so Paul and Carolyn stood on each side of her as she walked.

On stage, Justice was finishing what normally would have been his last song, but he had a surprise for his mother. The next day was Christmas, and it was her and his aunt's birthday.

Before he started his surprise, he looked on the front row for his mother, but she was missing. He panicked and scanned the room until he saw her about to exit through a side door.

"Nooo! She can't leave yet," he said to himself and immediately knew how to stop her.

Gracefully, Justice hit the E-flat chord on the baby grand piano, and after playing a few more notes, he saw his mom stop walking and turn around.

"Gotcha!" he said to himself while watching his mother take a few steps down the aisle so he could see she was listening. There was a faint smile on her face, but he could tell something was wrong with her. He continued to play in hopes of making her feel better.

Carolyn swayed her head to the most beautiful song she had ever heard. *It Came Upon A Midnight Clear,* it was her favorite Christmas song. Justice had mixed it into his playlist just for her. She looked to the left of the stage where the steps were and laughed at the upset look on Cali's face. He had obviously added the song behind her back, and from the looks of it, she was big mad.

"It came upon the midnight clear. That glorious song of old. From angels bending near the earth

To touch their harps of gold. Peace on the earth, good will to men. From heaven's all-gracious King!" she sang softly and placed one hand over her heart. She waved the other hand in the air so Justice could see she loved her surprise.

Although Paul and Marilyn fussed and tried to drag her out of the arena, her feet were planted in the same spot until her baby boy finished his birthday gift to her. When he hit the final note, she passed out.

IN LOVING MEMORY

CAROLYN JUSTINE LANDRY-BENOIT

Beloved Wife, Mother, Sister, Aunt,
and Extraordinary Humanitarian
12/25/60 - 12/24/95

Each one must give as he has decided in his heart,
not reluctantly or under compulsion, for God loves a cheerful
giver.
2 Corinthians 9:7

"Of all days, why would it rain on THIS day? I hate this! My mom didn't like rain. Why would God ruin it for her? He ruins everything!" Justice mumbled, removed his suit coat, and tugged at his tie. "I hate ties too, mama woulda never made me put a tie on."

He kicked rocks near his mom's grave and purposely stood outside the huge green tent so it would rain on him. His dad was so engrossed in the pastor's final words, he didn't notice his son standing in the rainy, cold weather. Fortunately, his aunt; Marilyn, saw him and motioned for her son; Kevin, to check on him.

"Hey lil cuz, come under the tent with us. It's raining mane," Kevin tried to get him to come out of the rain, but Justice was not having it.

"Leave me alone Kev, and stop calling me 'lil cuz', you ain't but 3 months older than me." Justice yelled at his cousin and angrily kicked muddy rocks his way.

Marilyn witnessed the incident and quickly jumped in. "J.B. Stop that! Right now! Come here! You gon' get sick boy! It's too cold for you to be standing in the rain." She pulled him close to her and gave him a hug. She then held him until the service was over.

When Justice saw his dad place a single white rose on his mother's coffin, he asked his aunt if he could do it too. She handed him a rose.

Slowly, he walked to his mother's coffin and gently placed the flower on top. Anxious to go home, he grabbed his dad's hand and tried to pull him towards the line of waiting limos.

"Come on dad, let's go! Come onnnn! Let's go home. Please!" he begged.

It didn't work, his dad's feet were planted at the grave. He refused to move.

Marilyn saw her brother-in-law staring at her sister's tombstone falling apart. She knew it would happen at some point but didn't know it would be at the burial. She told everyone to head to the Repast and leave Paul alone to say goodbye to his wife of fifteen years.

"Paul, I'm going to take Justice and Kevin with me back to the church in the limo. Here," she tossed the keys to her late-model Honda Accord, and he caught them.

"Bring my car to the church whenever you're ready. Take your time."

As she held the umbrella over her, Kevin, and Justice's head, she walked away. Seconds later, the cemetery workers started twisting the crank to lower the coffin into the ground. Paul dropped to his knees in front of the 6-foot hole and covered his face with his hands. He cried like a baby.

The sound of the crank almost broke Marilyn down as well. Her knees buckled, but she held herself together. Carolyn was her twin sister, so in that moment, she felt like half of her soul was being lowered into the muddy ground. To calm herself and be strong for her nephew, she hummed her sister's favorite Christmas song: *It Came Upon A Midnight Clear.*

CHRISTMAS EVE 2020

"Hello? Are you there? Justice did you hear me?" Charity asked while listening to the man she loved breathing in her ear, but not responding. She looked down at the phone to see if he was still on the line. He was.

Aggravated and fed up with his silence, she inhaled and exhaled to calm herself and her thoughts. She wanted to be sure she was in a rational headspace before she spoke again.

"Listen, J.B., you know I have loved you since you walked into Mrs. Grayson's Creative Writing class, Sophomore year," she laughed at the beautiful memory. "Everybody at Loyola said we had nothing in common, so they couldn't understand how we were friends. They said you were an asshole, and I had a heart of gold. What a mismatched pair we were… and still are… indeed," she laughed again. "The women all said you were difficult to deal with, and although you were the finest man on the yard, you couldn't keep a girlfriend even if Jesus paid you." Charity held back her laughter and allowed the tears to fall silently. "Justice, for as long as I can remember, I have shown you where my loyalty lies, yet you've never really been loyal to me. You always make me pay for what everyone else does to you. And it is clear now that you'll never really SEE me," she cried softly and held her breath as she waited for him to say something… anything. She held and held until she almost choked. Her refusal to exhale revealed her stubborn fear of the truth. He didn't love her… well… not in the way she loved him, and his silence proved it.

"I love you sooo…" she stopped herself, "You know what, I was about to say the same things I have said to you before… time and time again! You've even mocked me for being a broken record. I remember a few months back when you told me you didn't want to hear what I had to say because I say the same thing all the time. You then told me to move on with my life, and you said I would be back. That was very arrogant and mean of you Justice… VERY!" her voice rose, and the tears of sorrow turned into tears of anger. He finally spoke.

"If you raise your voice at me again, you know what I'm gon' do. I'ma hang up. I don't do the disrespect, you know that. Just like I told you before, I ain't stoppin' you from datin' or doin' whateva' you gotta do to make yourself happy. I don't own no property with you. I ain't married to you. And I ain't got no kids by you, so you're free to go to gotdamn Afghanistan or anywhere else you wanna go if that will make you happy. I don't care Charity. I really don't." He was done talking.

Charity was "smoking gun hot", but unlike many other times, she held her tongue and controlled her temper.

"Justice, I will bring the books over tonight. And after my event tomorrow, I am going to ask Archer Literary Agency to assign my account to another agent. I hope you understand. You're amazing at managing my literary career, but I can't do this. I've given you my energy for almost 2 decades. You just can't go into 2021. I don't want to start or end the year with stress. I will see you soon. Goodbye!" She hung up and went to her office to work on the changes to her latest book.

Justice listened for a second, thinking she was still holding the phone.

"Hello? Hello?" he said. Then he realized she had hung up on him. "That was different. She didn't call me an asshole or curse me out this time," he smirked and went back to flipping through Instabook. He had been scrolling through his social media feed and "liking" pictures of women he knew and wanted to get to know the entire time Charity was pouring her heart out to him. He felt slightly guilty about not really listening to what she had to say… slightly.

"Mane… she'll call back, she's been saying the same thing for years. She ain't goin' nowhere… besides… when she sees what I'm about to do with her new book: *All is Fair in Love…*" he smiled to himself, "She gon' feel bad about trying to leave me… again. Especially when she finds out I'm the one that took her book, flipped it into a screenplay, and gave it to Bill Thacker's wife. I bet she gon' stop all of that mess she keep callin' me with! She ain't crazy enough to let her emotions stop her from securing that bag," he said out loud and then dismissed Charity's cry for attention when an image appeared on his Instabook feed.

"Damn! Baby girl got some tig ol' bitties!" He immediately hit the "Like" button on an image of a woman who was dressed like a low-end stripper.

"This girl right here is fine as hell! Yeahhh… I like em like this! I'm finna comment on this one," he mumbled and typed a comment: *"Girl… You 'fine'!*

He then noticed that Charity had posted something in her Instabook Story.

"Mane, that crazy girl always run to social media to vent. That's why I don't mess with her like that, she's childish! I'm surprised she didn't block me this time," he laughed.

Although he was pretty sure the post was about him, and he

didn't want to see it, curiosity wouldn't allow him to ignore it. He reluctantly clicked into it and read:

Justice is Blind!

He smiled, "That's my girl! She's clever as hell! No one will know she's talking about me, and as long as she keeps it that way, she can say whatever the hell she wants," he paused and decided to join her in the game she was playing. After thinking for a few moments, he clicked into his Instabook page and typed the perfect response to Charity's Instabook post.

Charity Sweet Charity!

He grinned in satisfaction.

"She really is a sweet girl, and she nags me like my mom used to do," he laughed, "But I don't do sweet. I can run over her too easily. She ain't no challenge at all. I guess I want her to be a little more hardcore." He stopped himself. "Shit, I don't want that either. I don't really want no gangsta chick. Not at this point in my life anyway. Hell, I don't know what I want. I do know this though… All of them degrees she got must not mean a damn thing because she's stupid if she thinks I don't SEE her. She's beautiful as hell, and she's so selfless. That girl will give the shirt off her back to anybody in need." He paused, "Just like my mama. Her parents fo' sho' gave her the right name. Hell… even Stevie Wonder can SEE Charity, it's just that…"

Knock… Knock… Knock

A knock on the door halted his self-justification for his poor treatment of Charity.

CHARITY C. BINGHAM

I will always love him for the man I first met, but I will forever hate him for the man he became.

-Charity B.

"Period," she said to herself as she licked the tip of the quill pen and dipped it in the ink jar to put a period on the last sentence of her latest book.

She was a bit of an eccentric. She believed in things like four-leaf clovers, lucky rabbit's feet, and soul mates. So, as a tradition, she never typed the first draft of any of her books, she always wrote them on paper. She also used an old school quill pen with a huge black feather to write the last sentence of every book she wrote. Justice had given it to her for Christmas a few years back, so that made it extra special. All the initial manuscripts for her books were also written in green notebooks… lime green to be specific. She had experienced huge success in a short period of time, and she attributed it to her lucky quill pen, green notebooks, handwritten stories, and Justice's advertising and promotional genius. In her mind, her formula wasn't broken, so it didn't need to be fixed.

Charity Bingham was an international best-selling author. She had topped the New York Times best-seller list three times and was working on her fourth book. Unbeknownst to her, the fourth book somehow caught the attention of media mogul; Bill Thacker.

Thacker was the mastermind behind so many successful television shows that critics claimed he had the "Midas Touch". His "touch" took shows like *Boyfriends, White-ish, Powerless,* and *King Sugar* to the Emmys every year, so he was picky when it came to what show he would greenlight next. He refused to come down from his winning streak. Day after day, he combed through scripts and fielded calls from agents who tried desperately to get him to see their client's vision, but he remained unimpressed.

Well, at least until Justice slid his wife an advanced copy of Charity B's soon-to-be released book: *All is Fair in Love* at a networking event a few weeks before.

Bill's wife had been raving about the book since she cracked it open, and after reading it, he understood why. It was the realest shit he had ever read. At least that's what he told Charity's agent when he reached out to him a few weeks back. He immediately optioned the book's concept for a new television series. The show would even carry the title of the book.

As Charity closed the notebook, she decided to log back into her Instabook account and delete the post she put in her "story". To her surprise, Justice's "story" was lit up. He had written something as well. She clicked into and read:

Charity Sweet Charity

She smiled. "You damn right I'm sweet. Too sweet for your

blind and stubborn ass." She thought about the phone call with him earlier and lifted her head to the heavens.

"Lord, I know I am making the right decision by switching agents and walking away from him. He's toxic and selfish. I should've listened to everyone on campus when they told me he was self-centered and emotionally unavailable." She dropped her head. *"But God, I know another part of him. The part where YOU shine through his rough exterior. Justice can be sweet and thoughtful and encouraging and…"* She stopped. *"But it's rare he shows me those things. I'm just a fool in love with a fool."*

Charity pushed away from the massive oak desk in her home office and wearily stood. A box in the corner caught her attention, and she frantically glanced at her desk clock.

"10:00 PM. Damn! I got caught up in writing and forgot to take those books over to Justice's house," she stared at the clock again. "He's probably asleep. But… he gon' have to get up and get these boxes because they need to be put in the gift baskets for the women's shelters at 6 in the morning." She smiled and flipped the light switch off. She didn't care how late it was, she wanted her charity event to be amazing, just like it was the year before and the year before that.

Charity's mom had been killed by her stepfather when she was ten years old, so women suffering in domestic violence situations was an issue close to her heart. This was why every Christmas morning for the last twelve years, she treated women in abuse shelters in the city to a day of pampering.

Ring… Ring… Ring

Charity jumped at the loud ringing of her cellphone in the dark office. She had left it on the desk near her computer by mistake.

"Oh shit! That almost gave me a heart attack," she said while holding her chest and picking the phone up from the desk. She saw her sister; Grace's face flashing on the screen and immediately became frustrated. She answered.

"Hello."

"Hey sis! You already know what I want. Tomorrow is Christmas, and I know you got the thing for the women, and I am sooo proud of you for that, buuut, I miss my sister, and Caleb and Rachel miss their aunt C.C. sooo… please say you made up your mind. Are you coming to dinner? Oh… and what do you want for Christmas?" Grace asked without taking a breath. She finally exhaled.

Charity laughed at her sister's anxiousness, "Girl, calm down. I know I have missed the last few years, but I WILL be there this year. I miss ya'll too. I spoke with dad earlier, and he said he is going to go help Justice and the others put the gift baskets together in the morning. That helps a lot. And who calls somebody on Christmas Eve AFTER the stores are closed to ask what they want for Christmas? That's crazy sis!"

She held the phone away from her ear because Grace started yelling right after she mentioned Justice's name. She dropped her head in shame because she had given her sister the ammunition not to like him. She thought he was an asshole, and that she should have left him alone a long time ago.

"C.C. I thought you said he was no longer your agent. You can't keep doing that to yourself. Dude is a jerk! And he does NOT want you. And you're lucky dad don't know the whole story because he for damn sure wouldn't be over there helping that mane do shit! But it ain't none of my business. You're 'grown', so I digress. Anyway, will you have time to make the caramel pound cake for dinner tomorrow? No one can top yours sis."

Charity rolled her eyes as she listened to her little sister chastise her life choices, but she knew she was right about everything she said.

"Ok Grace! You know I know you're right! And just so you'll stop acting like YOU'RE the big sister, I already told him that I am switching agents right after the holidays. That way, I won't have to talk to him, or see him until I can deal with my feelings. Honestly, I don't know how long that will take, and the way I feel right now, I may just leave him in 2020 completely. I don't see us being friends… at all."

"Cool, that's what I wanna hear. You deserve better C.C., and God will send you BETTER as soon as you stop holding on to the past. Anyway, I gotta get a bath and put on my smell goods before my HUSBAND gets home from work," she teased.

"Bye Grace! You ain't gotta throw yo' HUSBAND in my face. God will send mine soon and very soon. And I made the caramel cake earlier. It's on the counter. Also… as far as my Christmas gift is concerned, I just want the women at the shelters to have peace of mind. That's it!" she smiled.

Grace smiled at her big sister's selflessness. She had always been that way.

"Yes, HE… WILL send you your husband sis! Yes, HE WILL… and it ain't no Justice Benoit," she said with an attitude and hung up before her sister could curse her out.

Charity stared at the phone and shook her head at her little sister's childish behavior. She then went to the kitchen to grab the second caramel cake that she didn't tell her sister about, grabbed her keys and headed to Midtown.

"*M*aybe this is Charity." He looked at his watch. "10:00. This should be her. It's getting late. Whoever it is must've slipped past security. Mane, how did they get in the building without my letting them in? That security down there is lazy!"

Knock... Knock... Knock...

"Ok! I'm coming. Damn! Hold your horses!"

When he made it to the door, he looked through the peephole. Someone had their finger over it, and he knew who liked to play those types of games.

"Kevin... cuz... I thought you was Charity. How you get up here? And why you ain't call first?" he asked as he swung the door open.

"Wassup lil cuz! Some fine big booty chick let me in..." he answered.

"What I tell you about that 'lil cuz' mess mane? Anyway, did you get at her?" Justice asked a question he already knew the answer to.

"You know me! Her name is Shante, and she real cool, she…"

"Hol up… how you know she cool? You just met her like… what? 10 minutes ago?"

Kevin dropped his head and looked up at his cousin sheepishly.

"Actually, she let me in the building three hours ago. She stay down on the 4th floor, and ummm," he rubbed his bald head, "And ummm…" Justice's eyes flew open.

"Bruuhhh… You hit that? She let you hit that? Y'all smashed… already? Whaaat? Y'all use somethin'? Mane, that was quick!"

"Oh God, here we go again with the judgment!" Kevin was annoyed with his cousin's accusatory tone.

Justice threw his hands up in surrender.

"Look mane, my bad! You know these broads ain't loyal, but I ain't gon' say nothin' else! Who you sleepin' with ain't my business, but if you start burnin' when you go piss later, don't say I didn't try to tell you. Anyway, why you up here? What you want?"

Kevin walked over to the couch and sat down. He was trying to figure out how to ask Justice for $400 when he already owed him $300.

Justice peered at Kevin because he knew what he wanted… money; as usual.

"I ummm…" Something on Justice's computer screen caught his attention.

"J.B."! Who dis? This yo' new woman? I guess she aight… well… in that sorta 'round the way girl' typa way. She look like she been through some shit too! She kinda ratchet! Nawww mane… she got on one of them one-piece wrestling suits them chicks be wearin' nowadays." Kevin looked up at Justice and fell out laughing, "YOU wrote that she was "fine" under her picture? Bruh, you slippin', anyway, I got something to ask you."

"Mane, you JUST called ME judgmental, and look at how you judged that girl. She ain't so bad lookin'. I know her, and she thorough as hell! Real loyal! That means more to me than her looks. Anyway, how much money you want? I know that's what you wanna ask me ain't it?"

"There you go with that "loyal" shit again! I swear bruh, you gotta let that street mentality go! And you ain't even from the streets. You a damn millionaire round here workin' for no reason, you crazy! Anyway, broads ain't gotta do no crazy or illegal shit for you, or be all ratchet lookin' and shit to be loyal. And she ain't gotta always be from the hood either. Oh… and why you always put them women through the ringer to prove their loyalty to yo' uckly ass, but you ain't loyal to nobody but YOU? I'ma leave that alone though… for now. And yes, I need $400. I ain't got all my child support this month. There's something else I gotta ask you too."

Justice walked over and closed his laptop so his cousin could stop being nosy. He then looked at him.

"You already owe me $300, so IF I gave you the $400, that's gon be $700. When I'm gon get my money back? ALL of it?" he asked and started tapping buttons on his phone.

"Honestly bruh, I can give it back to you when I get my income tax refund."

"Dude… that's in February! Hell no! I need $350 mid-January, and the other $350 at the end of January. That's the deal, take it or leave it! Pay me like you pay yo' rent and yo' other important bills. Don't be holdin' my money and piecing it back to me. You want it or what?" he asked with his finger hovering over the send button on CashApp.

"Mannnneeee… Ok! Send it! I'ma pay you back on time." A

few seconds later, he heard the clinking coins sound letting him know the $400 had been sent.

"Now that that's done, lemme point something out. Your ex-wife… The woman who is raping you for child support was NOT a hood chick, she's a high school principal, and she was NOT loyal, so your argument is dead to me. All my "hood" chicks as you call them, they got ya' boy's back, and I don't have to wine and dine them to get what I need from them. They mess with me because I'm a REAL dude. So… I like what I like, and I ain't got to justify that to you and nobody else," Justice said with finality.

"Facts! I hear you loud and clear! I'ma let it go, but I got one last question."

"Go ahead, and then you gotta get out. I'm workin' on the floor plan for all the beauticians showing up at the Minglewood Hall in the morning for Charity's women's event."

"I'm glaaad you mentioned her because that's my question. What about Charity? She ain't never asked you for nothin' bruh. She mess with you because you a 'REAL' dude too, and she's had your back too, even though you've been a real "asshole" to her for years."

"I knew you were going to bring her up! You always do! You act like her biggest fan and shit!" He paused and stepped over to stand directly in front of Kevin, "Lemme find out the reason you be all on her ass like that is because you want her. Bruh… Charity is OFF LIMITS!" his voice rose higher than he planned.

Kevin jumped off the couch smiling like a Cheshire cat.

"Ohhh! Charity is off limits? Why J.B.? Why? Y'all just work together. Right? Remember, she ain't hood enough for you. She don't stroke yo' ego like them 'bottom feeders' you like to have sex with do. Remember, she ain't gon' let you control her? And she is just as prideful as you are, so she never asks you for anything. And… you would rather be mean to her than actually SEE her for the good woman she is." He stood toe-to-toe with Justice and dropped a bomb on him.

"Charity is MY type anyway. I want a decent woman in my life right now, and she does not intimidate me. I ain't insecure about who I am bro, and I for damn sure can satisfy her thick ass!"

That did it! Justice shoved Kevin onto the couch and was about to punch him when he saw he was laughing at him. He realized his cousin's intention was to make him mad, so he stopped.

"Kev, I told you what Charity said about me not satisfying her that ONE time in strict confidence. I ain't tellin' you nothin' else. That was cold."

"Mane, my bad, it's just that she's just as brutally honest as you, so I thought it was cool that she told yo' arrogant ass the whole truth. You deserved that shit!" He glanced at the closed laptop and remembered something. "Oh… and I see you ain't BLIND?" he laughed, "Yeah, I saw Charity's Instabook post a little while ago. Y'all two are hilarious! And… cuz… of course she's my type… she's everybody's type but yours. But I wouldn't do you like that. Besides… I kinda think she's moving on anyway."

"Not that I care, but why you say that?" Justice asked and held his breath nervously.

"Welll…" Kevin rubbed his head and tried not to make eye contact. "I saw her last Tuesday. She entered the building at the same time I did, so I assumed she was here to see yo' uckly ass. We got on the elevator together and joked and stuff. When we got to your floor, I held the door open for her to get off first, but she motioned for me to go on. I was confused as hell because before I got off, I noticed that the light on the 10th floor was lit up. Anyway, I got off, and she waved at me as the doors closed."

Kevin paused to cut his eyes at his cousin. Just as he thought, Justice was breathing hard to suppress his anger.

"Keep talking. Don't stop now!" Justice started pacing the floor.

"That's pretty much it cuz! You know you look just like yo' dad when you mad right?" He laughed. "Chill mane, maybe it ain't no dude or nothin'. It could be one of her friends or somethin'... who knows!"

Justice paced back and forth as he thought about what Kevin said. He had not been living in the building long, and Charity had never been to visit him, but obviously she had friends in the building.

"Hmmm... I wonder if these 'friends' are male? And how she gon' come up here and NOT drop by to see me. I been askin' her to come check me out for a minute now. How the HELL she..."

"Cuz... calm down and sit down! You workin' yourself up for nothin'. Besides... we got other shit to discuss. Wayyy more important shit!"

"Look, Kev, can't you see I'm busy? Quit beatin' around the bush, what else did you come up here for?"

"Aight... I know when I ain't welcome. Lemme go drop some kids off at the pool first, and then I'ma tell you. I been holdin' this in since I got here."

"Mane... why you always come over here to doo in my toilet? Who does that nasty mess?"

Kevin rushed to the bathroom and Justice yelled after him.

"Spray that Poo Pourii stuff in the toilet BEFORE you use it. Charity bought that boughie mess for me awhile back. It works though." He went back to flipping through Instabook.

On the way from the bathroom, Kevin caught a glimpse of something in the sunroom. He had been to his cousin's condo countless times, so he knew it was there, but he never brought it up. It was a taboo subject in their family.

After using the restroom, he walked back to the front room. On the way, he thought, *"Maaaane… tomorrow is a big day for my mom. He can't keep doin' her like that. She don't deserve that. She stepped in and did the best she could do. Forget this… J.B. gon' stop this mess right now,"* Kevin said to himself when he passed the sunroom again. He stopped and cut his eyes from the sunroom to the front room where Justice was seated. He took a few breaths to prepare himself for his cousin's wrath and went to have a conversation he should have had years before.

As he walked back into the room, Justice looked up and hit Kevin with news that made him angrier. He shared his holiday plans with him.

"Kev, I've been thinking. I might fly to L.A. tomorrow night after Charity's Christmas thing. Ain't nothing going on here, so I might spend the next few days out there with Giselle. I ain't seen her in a few years, so….," he looked up at his cousin and saw the shock on his face. He continued… "Yeah… her and that clown she was dealin' wit didn't work out, so she want ya' boy back. She sent me a message on Messenger through Instabook. I didn't even remember I unblocked her, but I'm glad I did, I kinda miss her."

Kevin was pissed at what he was hearing. Giselle Jordan was Justice's ex-fiancé', and she was the worst thing that ever happened to him. She cheated multiple times and kept him on her emotional rollercoaster until she got tired of him. She then moved to L.A. and started dating a guy she met off a dating app. With no warning, she dropped Justice for a man she met in person one time and had only known for two months. Fortunately, she was nice enough to mail Justice the engagement ring back...

"J.B. I do NOT want to hear about that broad. Do what you

do with her, but I need to talk to you about something important."

"Damn... you still holdin' on to that mess about her? Let it go. I forgave her, so you most definitely should have as well. Anyway, what's up?"

"Well... as you know, tomorrow is my mama's birthday, and..."

Justice threw his hand up to stop Kevin from saying anything else.

"Cuz... I know more than anybody what tomorrow is, and more than anybody, I don't give a fu..."

"Say it J.B... please say it, so I can beat yo' ass for it. That's MY mama, and she is also the woman who moved alll the way the hell to Memphis and took us away from our friends and our life in New Orleans to help your dad with yo' black ass! So... like I was sayin', tomorrow is her birthday, and she's turning 60. I told you 2 months ago about her party tomorrow night in New Orleans, and I expect you to be there. I'm still in Memphis because I wanted to make sure you got on a plane. Sooo... I will need a couple of hundred more to book our tickets for tomorrow at 2. I can get a cheaper flight, but we would have to leave sooner, and it's on an airline we really don't mess with. Anyway, I know you got Charity's event, so you can't go earlier. Like I was saying, there is a Southwest flight leaving out at 2 with one stop. We'll get there in time to make it to the venue before the decorators and caterers. Oh... and it would really make her happy if you... well... if you, you know..." Kevin pointed to the sunroom.

Justice stared at his cousin blankly, and when he saw him pointing to the sunroom, he stood up and silently walked to the front door. When he got there, he opened it and locked eyes with his cousin. Kevin knew exactly what to do. Leave. He had worn out his welcome.

"I'm leaving... but you need to call me back to let me know

what to do about the plane tickets. If you don't call, I will take an earlier flight without you. And IF I get on that plane alone… don't bother calling me again. We ain't cousins no more after that, and I mean that shit. My mama deserves better than your selfish ass neglect."

As he walked past Justice, he shook his head in pity.

"Kev, I love Auntie Lyn, and I appreciate everything she did for me, so all I can say right now is that I will THINK about tomorrow night. I won't make any promises I probably won't keep." He slammed the door before his cousin could respond and walked to his sunroom to pull the door shut.

Kevin stormed down the hallway to the elevator. His head was all over the place, and he ran into Charity. Literally. He knocked her down, and she dropped the box of books.

"Kevinnnn! What is wrong with you? Watch where you're going!" She looked up at Kevin in annoyance. He immediately apologized.

"I'm sorry! I was just… just… anyway, let me help you with those books."

He got on his knees and gathered the books to put them back into the box. Charity helped him and then he helped her up from the floor.

Sensing his frustration, she asked, "What did Justice do to you now?"

"Maaannneee… he won't be at my mama party tomorrow night! He said him and Giselle…" He abruptly stopped when he realized who he was talking to. When he looked at Charity, he saw she had dropped her head. She heard him.

"It's ok to finish what you were saying Kevin. It's ok." She looked up and held back the tears that were threatening to fall.

"So, Giselle is back in the picture?" She thought about the way he talked to her earlier. "No wonder. It all makes sense now. He is always a bigger asshole to me whenever he meets someone new or someone from his past reappears. I'm used to it now." Tears fell.

Kevin felt like shit for telling her something Justice should have told her. Staring at one of the sweetest women he had never dated, he couldn't help but to reach out and hold her. He was shocked that she allowed him to do it. He held her tightly as she cried in his chest. For a moment, he forgot about his cousin and inhaled the sweet smell of the flowery fragrance she wore. Seconds later, they overheard someone clearing their throat. It was Justice.

He was walking towards the elevator with a bag of trash in his hand.

"So, I see you finally made it with the books?" He checked his watch and turned on the "asshole" switch inside of him. He then walked over towards the trash chute to throw his trash away. "It's almost 10:30, you shoulda called to see if I was still up. It's too late for business." He glared at Charity with disgust in his eyes. "Or are you here for someone else on a more personal level? Huh? Maybe someone on the… lemme see… 10th floor? Don't even answer that. You know I don't give a damn about what you do. I don't care. I just don't," he rambled, "Anyway, let me get these books." He stepped between Kevin and Charity and bent down to pick up the box of books. Completely ignoring his cousin, he walked back towards his condo and motioned for Charity to follow him. She hugged Kevin again and thanked him for being there for her, and like a trained puppy, she walked behind Justice.

When they made it to his door, Charity walked in first, and before he followed her, he looked back up the hallway at Kevin.

"Kinfolk, she gon' ALWAYS be mine. Even if I don't quite

know what I'm gon' do with her yet. Oh… and I thought about it, I can't make auntie's party tomorrow night. So, yo' broke ass better take that earlier, cheaper flight. Tell her I love her, but I've decided to go to L.A."

Kevin stopped in his tracks and calmly turned to the man who was more like a brother than a cousin, and said, "Cuz, I meant what I said. So, this is where I finally exit that pity party you've been throwing for 25 years. I can't do it anymore. We're no longer family. Goodbye Justice."

Kevin pushed the button on the elevator and used his phone to book the final flight to New Orleans for early morning departure. The elevator took so long to come, he was able to book the flight and schedule his Lyft ride from his house. He was determined to make his mom's sixtieth birthday the most memorable yet.

Justice tried to shake off the guilty feeling that was slowly consuming him.

"Why everybody always expectin' me to do stuff I don't wanna do? I don't like parties. That don't mean I don't love my auntie, and that don't mean I don't want to be family with them. I just don't wanna be bothered. I just don't." He looked towards the elevator and admitted the truth to himself.

"It's my mama's birthday too. They always forget that," he mumbled as he watched his cousin get on the elevator and walk out of his life forever.

JUSTICE K. BENOIT

"Wassup baby girl?" Justice walked into his condo and put the box on his kitchen counter. He then hugged Charity and held on to her like never before.

After a few minutes, she pulled away from him and spoke back. She was not moved by his upbeat behavior. She knew him well; it was fake, something was wrong. His smile and conversation were both forced.

Charity had known for years that Justice suffered from depression, but he didn't like to admit it. He would rather people hate him and walk away from him than seek the help he needed to understand why they couldn't stay. She knew his mom passed when he was a little boy, and his dad two years later, but he never shared the details. He also never talked about his aunt Lyn. All she knew about her was that she moved back to their hometown of New Orleans when Justice and Kevin left for college. She knew Kevin because he went to Loyola University with them, and they all hung out together. As she thought about Kevin, she smiled at the memory of the warm hug by the elevator.

"Maybe I shoulda paid more attention to Kevin. He's handsome and smart and…"

"Broke as hell!" Justice cut her off. Charity had been thinking out loud because she forgot whose condo she was in.

"Huh? Who's broke?"

"Kevin is. I overheard you going on and on about him, and I ain't hatin' on him or nothin' but…" He glanced at Charity and saw the turned-up lips and raised eyebrows expression on her face. He burst out laughing.

"Yes, I am… let me quit."

Charity smiled. "Thank you, sir. That was true hating you were doing right there Mr. Benoit. Anyway, you can dead those thoughts forming in your head, I would never date Kevin. I was just giving him credit where credit was due. That curly-haired, red-boned, slim body, Creole thang he got going on is sexy." She locked eyes with Justice. "But… I like my men dark as night, around 5'11, with muscles and a bald head shaped like a peanut." Charity saw Justice rub his freshly shaven head and blush. She also saw him start to fidget because her flirting was making him uncomfortable, so she decided to change the subject.

"Sooo… ummm… it's nice in here. I like it," she nodded her head in approval of his new Midtown condo.

"Thanks. But I'm sure you've seen the inside of these condos before. You ever been up here?" He was fishing for who lived on the tenth floor.

"Justice, please stop. I know Kevin probably told you he saw me awhile back. And just so you'll know, my friend Randall lives on the 10th floor."

"Ummm… is that a man or a woman? I'm just wondering because the name Randall can go both ways."

Charity had had enough of his prying into her personal life, especially when he hadn't said a word about L.A. and the "she-devil" he almost married.

"Ok. So, listen. I have signed all the books in that box. I have a surprise in the car for your mean ass, so, I'll go get it in a minute. Where are the ones you need me to sign?" She successfully changed the subject. Justice caught the hint and moved on.

"Ohhh ok. They're over there." He pointed to a box on his couch. "And thanks for the compliment on my spot. It's temporary though… just until I figure out if I am going to stay in Memphis. I been getting calls about some of my client's manuscripts, so, who knows, this might be my last year in the M-Town. If I can flip those manuscripts into a successful TV series or two, everybody gon' be callin' ya' boy about a new hit storyline, and since I don't write, that means ya'll… oops… I forgot, I ain't finna be your agent anymore." He smirked at Charity and continued with his dreaming. "So that means my OTHER client's stories are what I'm gon' be presenting to them. Yep, I think my Oscar will look good on that wall right there." He pointed to an empty space on the wall near the TV. Justice forced his excitement about possibly flipping his client's books into blockbuster movies. Truthfully, he didn't care about taking anyone to the next level except Charity. It was her dream. Not his. He was good at making the dreams of others come true, but his real dreams were dormant. God had allowed him to have a taste of them long ago, and he honestly missed the feeling of using his gift. But his guilt and pride wouldn't let him be happy, so he pretended to like being a literary agent.

"Yep. That golden beauty gon' say: Justice K. Benoit. Anyway, I'm over here trippin'." He laughed.

Charity wanted to be an asshole like him and ignore his talk about being more successful. He did her like that all the time. Things she was excited about were rarely of any concern to him. In most cases, she would call him excited and get off the phone feeling deflated. He always gave her responses that were dry and lacked any emotion at all. She often had to remind him that she was alive. But… as usual… she pushed what she wanted into the background in her own life and encouraged him. She loved him.

"No. You're not trippin' J.B. You're amazing at what you do." Charity looked at the empty space on the wall where he wanted to put his "make-believe" Oscar. "I agree. That would make a good spot for your award. "She paused and asked a question that had puzzled her for years.

"Justice. What does the 'K' stand for?"

"Huh?" he asked.

"The 'K' in your middle name, what does it stand for?"

He thought for a moment about his response as he stared into the sincerest eyes he had ever seen. They were second to none other than Carolyn Justine Landry-Benoit, his mother. Something in Charity's eyes told him he could tell her his secret. They had been friends for seventeen years, and she didn't know much about him because he was very private. But after what happened with Kevin, he wanted… no… needed, to unload the heaviest burden he ever carried… his past.

"Keys. My middle name is Keys. My mom grew up in New Orleans in a family with nine brothers and sisters, and her and my aunt Lyn, that's Kevin's mama… loved music." He smiled wistfully. "Well, my granddaddy used to play the piano better than Beethoven and Bach put together. He learned to play by ear. He had no training at all," he said proudly. "My mama and aunt, they were twins ya' know. They wanted to play too, and my granddaddy was determined to teach them. He always bragged about training his twin daughters on an old baby grand piano that my grandma bought. She worked extra hours to purchase it from the wealthy white family she cleaned for. Well, the story goes that they tried and tried, but they both had "butterfingers", he laughed. "That's what my granddaddy used to call them. My mama told me they wore that old piano out but couldn't play to save their lives. After a few years, they all gave up. They were convinced that my granddaddy was the only one in the family with the musical genes. So, when Kevin was born, my aunt Lyn gave him the middle name of 'Lyric', but don't tell him I told you that." He laughed again. "And when I came along a few months later, my mom gave me the middle name of 'Keys', both of our names were partly because of their love of music, but mostly because by then, my granddaddy had passed away. That is how they honored him. Anyway, life moved on and the old piano just sat in a corner in my grandma's house, but when she died, my aunt was living with Kevin in a tiny apartment, and my parents lived in a spacious home, so the piano came to our house." Justice was nervous about the next part of his story, so he went to the kitchen to pour himself a glass of wine to calm his nerves. He gulped the entire glass and leaned on his bar to push through the most painful part of his life.

"One day, when I was 4, I was coloring on the floor in the living room where the piano was, and I noticed that the keys were all nice and white." He threw his hands up innocently because he saw the look on Charity's face, she knew what he was about to say.

"No. You didn't! J.B. Nooo," she said while covering her mouth in shock.

Justice laughed out loud. "Yes. I did! Mane, I tried to make the white keys black like the other ones, but my little black crayon wouldn't work. So, my little bad ass went and found my dad's PERMANENT black marker and started drawing stick figures on the piano keys. My mama walked in that room and saw what I was doing, and she screamed like somebody was killing her or something. She tore my black ass up! I STILL remember the pain from that whooping." He winced from the memory and kept talking. Charity was loving every minute of his story. She felt special because he chose her to reveal such intimate details of his life.

"After the beating I got, my mama sat me at the piano and sat next to me. She said since I was so interested in her piano, then I might as well learn to play it. She told me where it came from and about my granddaddy. She then took her hands and placed them on top of mines and guided me across the keys. She admitted she couldn't play that well, but her dad was successful at teaching her and my aunt to play *It Came Upon A Midnight Clear* at Christmas time. She said because her dad was so excited they were able to play it perfectly, they played it every Christmas for him until the day he died. After she played it for me twice, the phone rang in the kitchen, and my mom left me at the piano to go answer it. I remember vividly that my mom was talking to my aunt Lyn because I heard her explaining what happened to our family piano. I sat on the bench feeling ashamed of what I did and trying to scratch the black off the keys I had marked up. The melody of the song my mom played for me kept playing over and over again in my head, and my little hands somehow knew which keys went with each note of the song. Before I knew it, I was playing *It Came Upon A Midnight Clear* flawlessly. My mom walked into the room with the phone to her ear when I was starting to play it for the second time. I looked up at her with my hands still on the keys, I didn't even need to look at the piano. I was playing from the melody in my head. She smiled, and I saw the tears fall from her eyes. I heard her tell my aunt: *'Lyn, I think I gave Justice the perfect middle name. And I know I didn't get daddy's ability to play the piano, but I for damn sure gave birth to a child that did.'*

"Waiiiit… Justice! I remember the little black boy from Memphis who was a child piano prodigy. That was like in the late 80's. The teachers at my school used to show us footage of him playing for people like Queen Elizabeth." Charity thought for a minute, "YOU'RE Justice Keys? WOWWW! I have never heard you mention the piano… AT ALL! Why?"

She was so excited to know his secret that she didn't notice he had gotten silent. When she realized it, tears were rolling down his face, and he was rocking back and forth.

"I wish I woulda never touched the piano that day at my parent's house Charity. It killed her! That damn piano and that stupid ass song. I shoulda let her go to the hospital. I shoulda let her go! My aunt shouldn't have listened to me. Why did she make my mama stay? Why come she didn't see my mama was too sick to stay for that stupid concert," he cried.

"No Justice No! You were just a kid. I am sure there was nothing you did wrong, and I am pretty sure your aunt didn't do anything wrong either. Stop blaming yourself. It ain't your fault. Baby look at me," Charity begged.

She had never seen him so vulnerable, and her heart hurt for him. She lifted his chin and wiped the tears away. She then leaned in for a kiss and Justice met her halfway. Their tongues danced in perfect harmony. They both stood up, still locked in the kiss, he took her hand and led her to his bedroom. Charity shook from nervousness because she didn't want him to change his mind. They had slept together before, but it was before he met Giselle. It had been at least five years since they did what she hoped they were about to do. She wanted him to make love to her more than anything else on earth, but his ringing phone halted everything. It was a Messenger call from Instabook, and it was like the unique ring tone snapped him out of a trance because he let go of her hand and ran to catch the call.

She stood in his doorway and watched him talking on the phone, hoping he would come back. He never did. When she looked up again, he was sitting on the couch staring at the computer screen. He turned to see her standing there and told her to come sit down.

"Hey, Charity, come on back out here. We got work to do." He looked at the clock on the wall.

"It's 11:00. We both gotta get up early in the morning so your

Christmas event will start on time. Come on and sign these books right quick. Your dad gon' still meet me and the team, right?"

Charity's spirit dropped. "I know he suffers from depression, but damn! Is he bi-polar too? Dang! God, I cannot keep doing this. I gotta be done after tomorrow. His ups and downs are killing me softly," she said to herself and threw her head back to cancel the tears that desperately wanted to fall.

She walked over to the couch as Justice got up to move to a chair. He wanted her to sit next to the books so she could quickly sign them and leave. He knew he almost made a huge mistake by sleeping with her, and his flesh and his heart wanted to pick back up where they left off before the phone call, but his mind knew he couldn't. Charity sat down and reached into the box to remove the books to place them on the coffee table. But when she set the first book down, she noticed a stack of papers with the name of her latest book on them. She reached for them.

"Yeah J.B. My dad will be there on time to help. What are these?" she asked.

"Uh uhn! What you doin'? Leave those alone. That's my personal stuff. Ain't nothin' on that table for you."

"But why do those papers have the name *All is Fair in Love* on them?"

"Look mane! You're signed with The Archer Agency, and for right now, I am your literary agent, so just know that I'm doing my job. Don't worry about those papers Charity. I gotcha."

"Ok... I won't touch your shit then sir," she said with an attitude.

Charity couldn't focus on signing the books anymore, so she sat in silence for a few minutes and let her overthinking get the best of her, as usual. She couldn't understand why he didn't want her to look at the papers. His secrecy always drove her crazy.

"You know what, I gotta go. I ummm... got something to do," she said after grabbing her keys and heading for the door.

Justice saw her get an attitude and didn't really feel like dealing with it, but he knew her like the back of his hand, so he had to smooth things over, or the Christmas women's event would be a disaster. She would be avoiding him at all costs, and that would make the day more difficult than he already anticipated it would be. Justice knew what he had to do.

"What I do now? Damn Charity! What's wrong with you? Stop. We gon figure this out," he looked at the coffee table and shook his head at the papers.

"Ohhh… I see! You think I'm hiding something from you? Girl, you know better than that!" He picked the papers up and tried to hand them to her. She refused to take them.

"Here. I'm trying to show you that I would never do anything behind your back. Take the papers and read them. I'm working on something big, and I didn't want to include you until I knew for sure. But… if it will make you feel better, read them."

Charity took the papers and placed them back on the coffee table without reading them. She stared at Justice lovingly and remembered the caramel cake in the car. It was his favorite, so she made one just for him.

"I trust you J.B. Look, I gotta go back to my car to get the other box of books I need to sign for tomorrow." She smiled. "Annnddd… remember I have a surprise for you!"

"Oh yeah! That's right! You know I like surprises! Cool, go head, be careful down there, it's…" He looked at the clock on the wall. "It's 11:15, and Midtown got some weirdos, plus, it's dark out."

Justice laughed and walked into the kitchen to pour himself another glass of wine.

"Really Justice? You gon' just let me..." Charity noticed he wasn't listening, so she continued to stare at him expectantly, but he ignored her and focused on his drink. Shaking her head in disappointment, she rushed out of the condo.

He watched her leave and thought about Giselle. She was the Messenger caller from minutes before, and although he cut the call short, he knew he shouldn't have answered it at all.

"Justice Benoit, you're always messing shit up!" He hit himself upside the head. "I am so confused right now! I don't love Giselle anymore. I don't even know if I ever loved her. She's just... just... hell... I don't know. She fine as hell though, but she's too clingy. She a freak too, a real nasty one." He bit his bottom lip lustfully. "But that don't make her wife material. She is also a liar, a cheater, and petty as hell. Plus, when I needed her, she turned her back on me. What was I thinking? Mane, as soon as Charity gets back up here, I'ma tell her why I'm an asshole, but shit, I don't even know the answer to that question. I got some loose ends to tie up, and Giselle is one of them. I can't pull Charity into my mess. I just need a little more time to figure this all out. Charity is sweet, she'll understand, she always does. I've done this to her before, and she was good."

Justice convinced himself that the solution to his problems was more time, and he was satisfied with that. Forgetting about Charity for the moment, he went back to flipping his computer screen from the floor plans for her Christmas event to Instabook.

CHARITY C. BINGHAM

Charity hurried down the hallway and stepped on the elevator while her thoughts played ping-pong inside her head. She didn't know if she should get the books and take them back up to Justice, or if she should just take them to her dad's house in the morning and avoid Justice at the Christmas event.

When she got off the elevator and walked out of the building into the dark and cold December night, she cautiously looked around. Justice's condo was off Poplar Ave. near the Overton Park area, and there were usually people walking their dogs or hanging out, but the night was eerily quiet. Charity nervously inhaled the cold air and pulled the belt to her coat tighter around her waist. She ran up the block to her silver, late-model Toyota Camry as quickly as possible. She was scared. She had no business being out at almost midnight alone.

When she reached her car, she had made up her mind.

"I promised 100 signed copies of my newest book to the ladies at the shelters, and I am going to keep my promise."

Charity clicked her keypad to open her car door and got the few books and the cake that was in the passenger seat. She then popped her trunk to grab the second box of books and put the cake on the hood of the car. She was going to take them back up to Justice. When she pulled the books from the trunk, she put them on the ground and reached into her pocket for the key to lock her car back up. The keys were not there. She kneeled to see if she dropped them in the box. They were not there either.

"What the hell? They were just in my hand! Where did they go?" Charity panicked and ran to look inside the car. They were still nowhere to be found. Suddenly, she heard dogs barking and cars honking, all the sounds she didn't hear at first. The night had come to life, and she felt a little better because she knew people were around somewhere nearby. She then looked at all the clothes and miscellaneous things in her trunk.

"Damn! My dad told me a few days ago to clean this thing out. I just didn't have the time. This is a mess! I bet I dropped my keys in here." She rolled her eyes at the junk in her trunk.

It was so full she couldn't see the carpet in the bottom of the trunk.

"Damn! I gotta take all this stuff out?" She took out her cell phone and looked at it.

"11:55… Maybe I should call J.B. to come help me." She thought, but her pride and stubbornness eclipsed her common sense.

"Nope! He shoulda never let me come down here by myself. I wonder how long it's gon' take him to come see about me. What kinda man sends a woman out into the dark like this?" Charity started crying because she knew he didn't care about her, but the longer she stood outside by herself, the more she was done with Justice Benoit. She needed to be pissed off enough to finally let him go… for good.

She wiped the tears from her eyes and slowly started removing every item from her trunk, starting with her lime green laptop bag.

JUSTICE K. BENOIT

"*D*amn! She don' got big as hell! Maybe she needs some of that laso Tea or whatever it's called that everybody on Instabook be tryna sell." Justice laughed to himself while trolling the page of a woman he went to high school with.

Pow! Pow!

"Damn! Not again. Somebody was shootin' last night too. I gotta get out of this area. It's always somethin' crazy goin' on over here," he said while ignoring the gunshots in the distance. All of a sudden, the lights blinked in his condo, and he heard what sounded like a piano playing. Justice was spooked because the melody was a song he had not heard in twenty-five years. It was *It Came Upon A Midnight Clear.* He knew he had to be hearing things, and he blamed it on the wine he had been drinking all night. Shaking the eerie feeling off, he tried to get back to trolling, but something felt weird. Justice got up and walked out on his balcony. He looked down on Poplar Ave. and saw a teenage boy with a red baseball cap and red sneakers running through the empty Walgreens parking lot. He was carrying a lime green bag.

"He sure is in a hurry! He must be late for curfew or something." He laughed to himself and went back in. Closing his balcony door, he noticed the door to his sunroom was slightly cracked. He clearly remembered shutting it earlier, but he blamed it on the wind.

Twenty minutes later, he thought about Charity and looked at the clock.

"12:25? She's been out there like an hour. I bet her moody ass left and didn't say shit. I'll just get the books in the morning. I'm glad she's switching agents. I can't deal with her anymore either. I can't seem to do shit right by her. I give up!"

He started to call her, but let it go and went back to finalizing the floor plans. His computer was locked from the inactivity, so he had to put his password in again. When it came back on, he saw something that made him jump off the couch. Scrolling across his Instabook timeline was a collage of Charity's books and one of her author headshots. Underneath her picture were the words:

R.I.P.
Charity B: #1 International Best-Selling Author
#gonetoosoon
#restinpeace

"Huh? Charity ain't dead! She's ummm… probably at home by now! People on Social Media are always killing folks. They need to stop making up shit! I don't even know why I keep getting on here." Angrily, he shut down his computer, and then his phone started ringing. When he looked at the image on the screen, he saw it was Kevin. He answered.

"I knew you couldn't stay mad at me for long cuzzo," Justice joked.

"J.B.? Where you at? You still at home? When did Charity leave from up there?" Kevin asked frantically.

"Cuz, stop tryna get at her. You ain't her type, she like dark chocolate," he joked again. "But yeah, where else I'ma be, it's after midnight, and I'ma 'old head' now, so I ain't doin' no clubbin'. And Charity's moody ass left like an hour ago. She mad at me again, so I'ma let her cool off and call her in the morning. Wassup? Why you sound so stressed?"

On the other end of the phone, Kevin cried soft tears and tried to figure out how to tell his cousin what he obviously didn't know.

"J.B. Come downstairs now. I'm in the lobby area. After we had words earlier, I went down to Shante's condo, so I never left the building. Just come down to the lobby. The police need to see you."

"The police? What you talkin' bout Kev? I don't mess with the police like that, and you know it. I ain't comin' down there if that's what you tryna get me to do. What they need me for anyway? Kev, what is going on? What are you not telling me?"

"JUSTICE!" Kevin yelled. "Just bring yo' ass downstairs. Damn!" He hung up.

Justice heard the urgency in his cousin's voice and grabbed his coat to head to the lobby area.

When he got down there, he saw police everywhere. He spotted his cousin talking to an officer, and when Kevin saw him, he motioned for him to join them.

"Officer, this is my cousin Justice Benoit, he was Charity B.'s manager," Kevin explained.

"WAS? I still am. What's going on down here Kevin?" He looked through the glass doors in the lobby area out onto the street. Something took over his body and pushed him outside. He didn't wait on a response from Kevin because he somehow already knew the answer.

Justice muted the noise around him and walked in a trance-like state through the lobby and out into the cold. When he stepped outside, that same "something" told him to turn left and walk up the block. He realized he was walking into the thick of the commotion when he saw news reporters and several police cars surrounding an ambulance and a silver vehicle. Blue and red lights swirled into the midnight sky together and made Justice dizzy. He swooned a bit as he got closer to the center of attention, but he kept walking.

Slowly, the silver car's make and model came into view. It was a Toyota Camry. He then witnessed the coroner zipping up a black body bag. His heart told him who was inside.

"Charity sweet Charity! Nope. No way!" he said to himself as reality fought with disbelief inside his mind. Refusing to believe the truth, he reached for his cellphone to call Charity.

He found her number in his phone, and her face showed up on the screen. He took a moment to stare at her beautiful smile, and just when he was about to hit send to call her, something on the ground near the trunk of her car caught his attention. It was a box of books, and next to it flipped upside down in the container, was a caramel cake.

"The books! And the cake must've been my surprise! She makes the best caramel cakes!" he said as reality won the fight in his mind. He then screamed louder than he knew he could. "Aghhhh! Oh God! Oh God! Not again! This is all my fault. I shoulda came and got the books myself. What the hell kinda man am I? I ALWAYS ruin everything. He looked up to the dark sky. No. YOU always ruin everything! I was trying. I just needed more time Lord. Why couldn't YOU let me get myself together before you took somebody else away from me." He didn't care that everyone was watching him break down. He was tired of feeling like he couldn't do anything right. Several officers tried to approach Justice for questioning, but Kevin blocked all of them. He told them that he would have his cousin reach out to them in an hour or so.

"J.B. Let's go inside. Ain't nothing you can do out here. We can figure this thing out together, but it's cold out here," Kevin said calmly as he squeezed Justice's shoulder to show his support.

Justice aggressively pushed Kevin's hand away and turned to face him.

"No! WE… ain't gon' figure shit out TOGETHER! WE ain't family no more! Remember? Kevin, leave me the fu…" He stopped himself when he remembered the young boy running away, the red baseball hat, the green bag, and the red sneakers. He pushed Kevin out the way and walked towards the nearest officer.

"Officer, look… Ms. Bingham was in my condo before this happened. She came out to get those books." He pointed to the box. "When she got out here, somebody obviously robbed her." He dropped his head in shame. "I heard gun shots around midnight. But I didn't think that…. Anyway, I got up to look over my balcony, and I saw a young boy, in red sneakers and a red baseball hat, carrying a bright green bag running across the Walgreens lot over there." He pointed across the street as the officer wrote down the details.

"Did you say bright green bag?" An older man asked as he walked over to Justice and the officer.

The officer motioned for the man to step away from the crime scene, but Justice spoke up.

"No officer. He SHOULD be here. He's Ms. Bingham's father. Hello Mr. Bingham."

"What the hell happened to my daughter Justice? I got a text from a friend of mine saying they saw her face splashed across a breaking news story. I turned on the news and found out my child was dead. She told me earlier that she was bringing some books to you, so why in the hell was she out here alone? Where the hell were you, young man? And what did you just say about a green bag?"

"I messed up sir!" he cried. "I wasn't paying attention, and I was working on the floor plans for her Christmas thing, and she got mad at me, so she went to get the books, but I didn't stop her, I shoulda stopped her. It's all my fault," he cried louder.

"Boy, pull yourself together. This ain't the time for alla that. Now, tell me about the green bag. It's important, hurry up!" Mr. Bingham insisted.

"Well… Ummm… a teenage boy was running with a green bag across the lot over there." He pointed to the Walgreens parking lot again. "It was like 30 or 40 minutes ago."

Mr. Bingham dropped his head, "I'll bet dollars to donuts it was my daughter's laptop bag that lil punk was running with. I told her 2 days ago to clean that damn trunk out and take that ugly green bag in her house." Mr. Bingham stepped over to Charity's open trunk. "The bag ain't in here I see."

The officer heard Justice and Mr. Bingham's conversation and laughed to himself at something the teenage boy might not have thought of.

"Sir, if that green bag was indeed your daughter's, and it actually had her laptop in it. We can trace the laptop, and I know it won't bring her back, but we may be able to get whoever did this to her. Do you have her account access code? Password or something?"

"I don't but hold on." He dialed a number and waited until his daughter picked up. She started screaming into the phone before he could get his words out.

"Callllm down Grace! I know baby, I know! Yes. She's gone. No. Ain't nothin' you can do here. But I do need C.C.'s password to her laptop. Do you have it? Yes, the Apple one you bought her for Christmas last year, with that ugly loud green bag! I'll tell you why I need it later. Just give it to me."

He waited on his daughter's response. "1-16-85? Why that date?" he asked.

Grace told her dad the significance of the date, and he glared at Justice.

Justice's eyes popped open when he heard Charity's password. It was his birthday.

Mr. Bingham gave the officer the password.

"Thanks sir, this will make finding her killer a lot easier. We hope. We've also nailed down the time of death as approximately midnight." He looked at his watch. "And it is about 12:40 now, so he couldn't have gotten far, especially if he was on foot." The officer looked over his notes again. "So, just to be sure. We have a black, teenage boy, with red sneakers, and a red baseball hat. Possibly in possession of a lime green laptop bag and laptop. Is that correct?" He looked up into the annoyed faces of Justice and Mr. Bingham.

"With all due respect, you asshole! He never once said the boy was black. I heard his recollection of what he saw, so how bout you ask him what color the boy was first, before you make that ignorant assumption!" Mr. Bingham angrily demanded.

"Oh. Sir, I'm sorry. It's just that… that…" The officer was at a loss for words, so he did as the older man asked him to do.

"Ummm… Mr. Benoit, what color was the teenage boy?"

"He was white. I know this because of the blonde hair that stuck out of the baseball cap, and I clearly saw his legs. It's like 30 degrees out here, and that idiot had on a gray hoodie and khaki shorts."

"Ohhh k. I think I got everything I need for now. Oh. Wait. Sir, does your daughter have a middle name? We have her ID. It was in her jacket pocket. So… we have her name as: Charity C. Bingham. What does the 'C' stand for?"

"Yes officer. It is Carolyn and write my number down too." Mr. Bingham rattled his number off to the officer just in case they needed to call with more questions.

"Carolyn… just like my mama. Damn! I never knew that." Justice mumbled to himself.

"Thanks sir. I think I got what I need. Here is my business card." He handed his card to Mr. Benoit. "Oh, and there are cameras in the Walgreens lot, so officers are over there now viewing the footage from tonight."

The officer walked away.

Mr. Bingham turned his attention to Justice.

"Walk with me," he said to him, and walked away. It was clear he expected Justice to follow him, and he did.

"Son, I'm assuming guilt is eating your ass up right now?" He looked Justice in the eyes.

"Yes sir! I feel like shit!"

Mr. Bingham saw the coroner's van leaving the crime scene. Overcome with anger, he grabbed Justice by the shoulders and forced him to watch the van leave with his eldest daughter's body inside.

"Yeah, you SHOULD feel like shit boy! But MY child don't feel like nothin', and she never will again. She's dead! Dead, you hear me? You see that van leavin don't ya'? That means I got ONE gotdamn child left. ONE! And I'm supposed to have TWO. You know why I ain't got two no more? Well, lemme tell you why son… It's because YOU ain't no man! You shoulda came out here yo' damn self and got that box. Yo' daddy didn't raise you right! You're selfish boy… just plain old selfish!" Mr. Bingham yelled and shook his head at Justice in pity. He then walked away to call the funeral home. He had a funeral to plan.

"My… my daddy didn't raise me at all sir. I was 12 when he died, so he never got to the 'manhood' part of my life. My mama dead too." He looked at the time on his cellphone. "And today is her birthday," he whispered behind Charity's dad. Of course, he didn't hear him.

"I'm so alone! I ain't got nobody. Nobody!" he mumbled to himself and noticed that Kevin was still lingering around the lobby. When he walked in the building, he passed his cousin and stopped to repeat what he mumbled.

"I ain't got NOBODY!" he said to his cousin and headed for the elevator while turning his phone off. He did not want to talk about Charity or what happened to her anymore that night.

Kevin watched Justice walk away and decided to leave him alone. He knew his cousin loved Charity, but he had always been too caught up in his own head and stuck in the past to admit it.

"Lil cuz, I pray things get better between us. And you're wrong! You always got me and my mama." He looked up to the sky. "Auntie Carol, please help your son. He needs you."

"I got him nephew! I got him!"

A soft, angelic voice whispered in Kevin's ear, and he almost jumped out of his skin.

"What the hell was that?" He knew the voice well, but he hadn't heard it in twenty-five years. "No way! Ain't no way! I'm hearing things! Lemme get my ass on to the airport. I'm glad I was able to get the last ticket on this late-night flight to N.O. I just hate it was with this triflin' ass airline. I spent all my money on my mama party, and everything else was booked and over-booked. Oh well, lemme get on out of here. I was waiting to the last minute to see if I could convince Justice to do the right thing, but it just ain't in him." Kevin remembered the ghostly voice and ran to his car. He almost tripped over his own feet. He couldn't get out of Midtown and Memphis fast enough.

Justice entered his condo and went straight for the liquor cabinet.

"Tennessee Whiskey. Old No. 7," he read the label on the bottle of Jack Daniels he chose as his poison for the night. He then reached into his refrigerator for the bottle of Coke but changed his mind and decided to drink the whiskey straight… from the bottle. One bottle turned into three, and he found himself sloppy drunk dancing around his condo.

"Alexa. Play *Swimming Pools* by Kendrick Lamar," he commanded.

The words to one of his favorite songs came bursting through the surround sound speakers, and he held his third bottle like a microphone while jumping up and down on his couch pretending he was on a stage.

"Pour up… Drank… Headshot… Drank. Why you babysittin' 2 or 3 shots. I'ma show you how to turn it up a notch. First you get a swimming pool full of liquor and you dive in…" he rapped.

As he was sliding into the next verse of the song, Kendrick Lamar's voice faded into the sound of a piano.

"Alexa. Fix that shit! That ain't what I asked you to play. Forget it! Alexa. Play *Drinkin' Problem* by Midland.

Justice jumped down from his couch and slipped on the rug. He hit the floor. He was so drunk, he remained there and kept singing along with one of his favorite country music groups.

"People say I got a drinkin' problem, but that ain't no reason to stop."

Once again, the song faded into the sound of a piano.

"Alexa. Cut it out! he screamed, but this time, the piano sound continued defiantly.

"Alexa stop!" Suddenly, everything went silent. Dead silent.

Justice struggled to get up from the floor, but finally made it. Slowly and softly, the piano sound started again, but it was not coming from the speakers. It was from somewhere inside the condo, and it sounded like a live performance instead of a recording. He stumbled around his condo trying to locate the source of the sound. He wobbled towards his bedroom and noticed the double doors to the sunroom were wide open. He knew he was drunk, but he was sure he closed the doors earlier in the night. He had also found the source of the piano sound. Normally, he would have been afraid to investigate the mysterious piano playing, but he was full of "liquid courage", so he boldly walked into the sunroom and stood in the middle of the floor. The room was empty except for a wooden clock on the wall, and a large, sheet-covered object in the corner. The sound was coming from underneath the sheet. He glanced at the wall clock, and the music stopped.

"12:00? That's impossible! It's at least after 1 AM. That clock must still be on Daylight Savings Time or something." He stumbled back into the front room to look at the clock in there.

"12:00? Hell nawww!" He powered on his cellphone to look at the time.

"12:00? What is going on?" he asked himself. The piano playing started again, but unlike the other times, the melody was distinct.

It came upon the midnight clear
That glorious song of old
From angels bending near the earth
To touch their harps of gold

Tears that had been locked up for twenty-five years flowed freely down Justice's cheeks. The music was soothing, he was drawn to it. He walked back to the sunroom and stood in front of the sheet-covered object. Rocking back and forth, he peacefully listened to the melody from underneath.

The world has suffered long;
Beneath the angel-strain have rolled
Two thousand years of wrong
And man, at war with man, hears not...

"It's being played in the key of A on the Treble clef. It's ok. But I like it in Bass clef in the key of B flat. It's wayyy better." He smiled. "Mama used to always play it on the Alto clef in the key of E flat. We would always argue about which version was better," he said aloud.

Justice listened to the melody with his face scrunched up because he desperately wanted to change the key. He couldn't take it anymore. He reached out and removed the sheet to reveal his family's old baby grand piano. The music stopped.

Gently, Justice caressed the wood and eased down on the rickety bench. He placed both hands on the keys and used his right hand to trace the black marker stick figures he drew when he was four years old. The piano started playing again. Right before his eyes, the keys were moving by themselves, but he was not afraid. This time, the song was being played on the Alto clef in the key of E flat.

"Mama?" he softly cried.

"Yes. Keys," she called him by his middle name as she continued to play *It Came Upon A Midnight Clear.* Slowly, she appeared next to Justice at the piano.

"Mama. You know Bass clef and B flat are better right? Come on now, we've had this argument time and time again. Move over and let the 'piano prodigy' do it. You know you got 'butterfingers'" Justice joked.

"Ok now... You ain't too old to get the same whoopin' you

got when you messed up my daddy's piano, 'Mr. Piano Prodigy'", she laughed and stopped playing.

"Play for mama Keys."

Mrs. Benoit rose from the piano and leaned over the side to watch her "pride and joy" play her favorite song. But he surprised her.

Happy Birthday to you
Happy Birthday to you
Happy Birthday my beautiful mommy
Happy Birthday to you

"Baby, you remembered?" Mrs. Benoit cried softly and leaned over to kiss Justice on the forehead.

"I could never forget your big day mama. I've remembered, and I say happy birthday to you in my prayers every year on Christmas." He looked up at her with hopeful eyes.

"Thank you for remembering, but I hope you say Happy Birthday to someone far more important than little ol' me on this day." She pointed up to the sky, smiled, and winked.

"Yeah… About that! I kinda… ummm… don't know how I feel about HIM right now. I used to pray all the time, but he never answered my prayers. Mama? Do you hear my prayers? You know… Up in Heaven?"

"Yes. Baby I hear and SEE everything you do." She cut her eyes at her only son.

Justice removed his hands from the keyboard and lowered his head in shame.

"Keys, that's why I'm here tonight. I understand that you're upset with God for taking me away. I saw that you couldn't even mourn for your dad because you never moved past my death.

Sweetie, I have been watching you mourn for me for far too long, and I want you to know that I am fine. As you know, your dad joined me 2 years after I went to Heaven, and although I would have liked for him to stay here to watch over and guide you into manhood, I love having the love of my life with me every day. I want that type of love for you. But to have that, you gotta move on baby. You're still that little boy who played the most amazing rendition of his mama's favorite song on that great big stage, dressed like the cutest wittle penguin ever." She pinched his jaws and laughed. " You're still that 10-year-old boy in your mind. You gotta let what happened that night go. You MUST."

"Mama. I've tried, but everything I touch turns into a disaster. I can't seem to do anything right. I'm the reason you died. And tonight, my friend Charity was killed because of me. I just need to stay in the house away from everyone. It's better off this way," he reasoned.

Mrs. Benoit did not respond to what Justice said. She simply told him to play.

"Play for mama Justice."

"Huh? Mama. I don't really play the piano anymore."

"Play for mama Justice," she insisted.

Not wanting to disappoint his mother, he started playing a melody of songs he had heard over the years.

Somehow, the music was amplified. It was louder and more beautiful than ever, and it sent Justice into a euphoric state. He closed his eyes and played effortlessly.

DECEMBER 22, 1995

When Justice opened his eyes again, he was in what appeared to be a doctor's office. His mother was standing next to him, but what was odd was that the woman sitting on the table being examined was his mother as well. He was confused.

"Pay close attention, Justice. Just watch," his mother urged.

"Mrs. Benoit, you've got to take it easy, your headaches are getting worse and worse. I strongly suggest you tell Paul what's going on."

"Dr. Patterson, we've had this conversation before, and I have the same answer for you. "No! I will be fine. Only 40% of patients with brain aneurysms have problems, and I am a praying woman, so I fall in the 60% category that will be just fine. Justice is playing at the FedEx Forum in a few days, and I am so proud of my little 'Keys". He has played all over the world, but he has never played in his hometown, so he is sooo excited to play in front of his friends and classmates. I just want to be there for him."

Dr. Patterson frowned at Mrs. Benoit's decision. "Mrs. Benoit, if you don't have the procedure tomorrow like I REALLY need you to, you won't be able to be there for Justice in the long run. I beg of you, please sacrifice this performance for the hundreds of others to come.

Skipping over his warning, Mrs. Benoit told the doctor what her plans were.

"Ok. I promise I will tell Paul right after Justice's performance, so you can schedule me for the procedure the day after Christmas. I want to enjoy my birthday, and then I can deal with all this medical stuff. Ok?"

"Mrs. Benoit, I don't think you can wait. Your vision is too blurry, the headaches, and the stiff neck you…"

"Stop it Dr. Patterson! I know all of that, but I am NOT going to miss Justice's FedEx Forum performance or my birthday celebration. My sister and I throw a party to remember Christmas night every year. So… bottom line. Sorry! I will see you the day AFTER Christmas."

Mrs. Benoit hopped off the table and walked out of the doctor's office.

"MAMA? You knew you had a brain aneurysm? Why didn't you say anything? Why did you keep it from dad? See… that's what I was talking about. You shoulda had the procedure to save your life, but my piano mess wouldn't let you. It's my fault. What did you show me this for? It made me feel worse."

"Honey, no. It was because of your piano playing that I was able to be around for as long as I did. The music was sooo soothing to me. It eased my headaches a lot. And even if I didn't come to your performance that night at the Forum, wherever I would've been, I would've had the same outcome. After I died, the doctor's told your dad that I was pretty much on borrowed time from the moment they found the aneurysm. I just wanted to live a normal life. No special treatment or looks of pity. I shoulda looked into the headaches long before I did. Justice, mama didn't take care of herself, and that is NOT your fault sweetie. DO you understand me?"

Justice nodded at her to let her know he did. When he looked back at the doctor's office, to his surprise, the room had turned into the bottom floor of the FedEx Forum.

CHRISTMAS EVE 1995

"Paul, is she ok? Has the headache gotten worse?" She looked at her sister and knew the answer to her questions. Carolyn's light complexion was fiery red. If "fever" were a person, her sister would be the face. Marilyn knew her twin was sick, and something inside of her told her that the headache was far worse than what she was telling them.

"I'm sorry Justice, I gotta break my promise. I agree with your dad, your mom must go now. She can't wait," Carolyn said to herself and started helping her brother-in-law with her sister.

Justice watched the scene up close and heard everything his aunt said. He looked over to his mother with tears in his eyes.

"Mama. I've been mean to auntie Lyn all these years because I thought she did what she promised she would do. I thought she made you stay even though you were sick. I thought she stopped you from going to the hospital." He became angry and punched the air. "It was all on me. I know. I knew it then too. I just needed somebody else to be the blame with me. I'm the one who stopped you. I'm so sorry mama. Sooo sorry!" He buried his head into his mother's chest and cried.

"Justice. It didn't matter how long I stayed that night. Even if

I made it to the hospital, I wouldn't have made it out of there. My aneurysm bursted, and there was nothing anyone could do. Baby, I passed listening to MY son, 'world renowned piano prodigy' playing the biggest venue in Memphis," she said proudly. "I went out in style. Babbyyy, I sang and danced my way right on into Heaven, and I've been dancing ever since."

Justice smiled when he saw his mom wiggling her hips and moving her feet to *It Came Upon A Midnight Clear.* He looked up on the stage and saw the ten-year-old him playing his little heart out trying to make her not leave the building. He then looked up the aisle near the Exit door and saw his mother smiling and swaying to her favorite Christmas song.

"Mama, thank you for bringing me back here, but I wanna go now. I know what's about to happen next, and I know I gotta let it go, but I can't stand here and watch you hit that floor again mama. I can't watch you die. Please! Let's go!" he begged and squeezed his eyes shut as he heard "little Justice" flowing into the final note.

When Justice opened his eyes again, he was sitting in the front room of his condo in front of the TV. He looked around for his mother. She was gone.

"Maybe I was dreaming." He looked down at the three empty bottles of Jack Daniels on the floor.

"I know I was drunk, so I probably imagined everything. Yeah! That's what happened." He reached down to pick up the empty bottles to trash them.

"I will stick to wine from here on out."

The strange dream he had about his mother was more sobering than coffee would have been, so he was wide awake. He tried to convince himself that he had fallen into a drunken slumber earlier, but something kept nagging at his soul.

Justice remembered he first saw his mother in the sunroom, so he wanted to at least check to see if the piano was uncovered. Before he could stand, the TV came on, and a breaking news broadcast was on.

"What the hell? The TV is glitching again. I gotta get that fixed. Alexa, turn the TV off." The news report continued.

He stood up to turn it off, but an image of the Memphis International Airport caught his attention.

"What's going on there?" he said and walked closer. "A plane went down in Lake Pontchartrain that departed from Memphis International. They sayin' that's all they know right now. Damn! They musta been headed to N.O. On Christmas Day! That's sad. Well… I hope they all survive," he said to himself. The TV finally went off, and he rushed to the sunroom. When he made it there, his mom was nowhere to be found. Oddly, the piano was uncovered, just as he remembered. He ran back to the front room but stopped in his tracks when he saw the door to his condo open. Seconds later, Charity walked in.

"What the fu…?"

"Justice Keys Benoit! If you finish that word, me and you gon' have a problem," his mother warned.

His eyes flew open.

"Mama? You still here? I thought… I thought I was dreaming."

"No son. You're more awake now than you've ever been in your life."

She pointed to his front door.

"Charity! Mama, that's my friend Charity," Justice yelled with joy. He rushed over to hug her, but his mom stopped him.

"No Justice. Just watch."

He anxiously stood by and watched the woman he thought

he'd lost forever pace back and forth. She looked sad and lost, he could tell she didn't want to be there. He also noticed what she was wearing and remembered she had on the same outfit when she visited him earlier in the night. Before she was…

"Ma. What's going on? Charity died tonight! How is she here?"

"Shhh," his mother said and told him to watch what was happening.

The door was still open, and he had a feeling about what was going on in the hallway. Curiously, he walked to the door to see if he was right. When he peeked outside and saw Kevin by the elevator, he knew exactly what was going on.

He was startled when he turned to look "himself" in the face, but he was more concerned about the mean things he was saying to the cousin who had his back when no one else did.

"Kinfolk, she gon' ALWAYS be mine. Even if I don't quite know what I'm gon' do with her yet. Oh… and I thought about it, I can't make auntie's party tomorrow night. Tell her I love her, but I'm going to L.A."

Kevin stopped in his tracks and calmly turned to the man who was more like a brother than a cousin, and said, "Cuz, I meant what I said. So, this is where I finally exit that pity party you've been throwing for 25 years. I can't do it anymore. We're no longer family. Goodbye Justice."

As Justice watched how nonchalant he was to Kevin, he made up his mind about something people had said about him for years.

"Damn! I AM an asshole!" he shook his head in disappointment and walked into the condo behind "himself".

"Himself" was carrying the box of books inside, and when he placed them on the kitchen counter, he pulled Charity into a hug. *The incident with his cousin bothered him more than he wanted to admit, so he held onto her like never before. He needed to feel loved, and hands down, Charity Bingham loved him if no one else did.*

"Mama. This was earlier tonight. She came over to give me

those books and to sign the books I had for her women's day tomorrow."

"Uh huh! But more than that happened. Didn't it son?" his mother asked, but was not interested in an answer, instead, she told him to keep watching.

As he watched, he saw "himself" and Charity kiss. He smiled at the recent memory because he had always been attracted to her, but for some reason, he always skipped over her and pursued other women. However, he flirted with her every chance he got. The kiss was explosive, and he remembered wanting to do it again and again and take her to his bedroom and... but Giselle called, and everything went downhill from there.

He placed his focus back on "himself" and Charity.

"I trust you J.B. Look, I gotta go back to my car to get the other box of books I need to sign for tomorrow." She smiled. "Annnddd… remember I have a surprise for you!"

"Oh yeah! That's right! You know I like surprises! Cool, go head, be careful down there, it's..." He looked at the clock on the wall. "It's 11:15, and Midtown got some weirdos, plus, it's dark out."

Justice laughed and walked into the kitchen to pour himself another glass of wine.

"Really Justice? You gon' just let me..." Charity noticed he wasn't listening, so she continued to stare at him expectantly, but he ignored her and focused on his drink. Shaking her head in disappointment, she rushed out of the condo...

"Nooo! Don't go Charity. Pleeeaaassseee don't go down there." Ignoring his mother's wishes, he rushed over to stand in front of the front door. He tried to block her from going out the door, but she walked right through him.

Justice then ran over to "himself" and yelled, "Get up! Boy! Don't let her go down there! Stop her man! Stooop herrr! Something bad is about to happen! Please stop her!" He waved his hands in front of "himself", but he was invisible. "Himself" just kept scrolling through social media completely oblivious to what was about to happen.

Not willing to give up. Justice screamed and cried and tried to run outside to bring her back, but there was a barrier at the door. He turned to look at his mother in frustration.

"Mama, I need to get out of here. Maybe I can bring her back inside. Why can't I leave this apartment? Please mama please!" he cried and begged.

His mother watched him in pity. "Baby, you can't go anywhere without me. I would have to take you outside, and I don't think…"

Pow! Pow!

"Nooo mama! Nooo!" Justice screamed as he ran to the balcony. A minute later, "himself" walked out onto the balcony as well, and they both witnessed the teenage boy in the red baseball cap running across the Walgreens lot with the lime green bag.

"Heyyy stop! That's not yo' laptop. I know what you did! I'ma find you! You're a dead boy running! Just wait til I find your ass! Stop motherfu…"

"Justice? Don't say it. And come back in here," his mother pitied him, but she knew his attempts were futile. Charity had passed through the heavenly gates moments before.

Justice dropped to his knees. He felt the pain of losing her all over again and became too weak to stand. His head was buried in his hands, and he was rocking back and forth bawling like a baby.

"I sent her to her death. I will never get over this pain. Her father hates me, he said I was not a man! He blames me too. He's right! This is more than I can bear mama! It's too much."

Mrs. Benoit kneeled next to her only child and hugged him tightly.

He nuzzled into her arms and cried himself into a gentle sleep.

A blast of below-freezing air whooshed past a sleeping Justice and forced him out of his peaceful nap. When he opened his eyes, his mother was gone, and his location scared the life out of him… literally.

He was laying in the snow in the middle of a "city of the dead". Miles and miles of above-ground tombs surrounded him.

"Aghhhh!" he screamed while trying to shield himself from the brutal cold air. He stood and wrapped his arms around his body, shivering. He looked around for his mother, but quickly realized he was alone.

"I'm in New Orleans! How did I get here?" He thought for a moment. "Mama? Why here? I get why you showed me everything else, but why here? Why?" he screamed.

No response.

Justice stood in the same spot he woke up in, for what seemed like hours. It was only fifteen minutes.

He inhaled and exhaled. Slowly accepting his circumstances, he looked around again to see if he could find the entrance. No Luck. He chose a direction and started walking.

"Maybe if I go this way, I will find somebody to lead me outta here."

As he walked, he couldn't help but to admire the beautiful displays of concrete and iron. He had to admit that although he was in a cemetery, the tombs had him awe-struck.

He started reading the names: Herbert, Broussard, Fontenot, Guidry, Boudreaux, Landry…"

"Landry?" He stopped when he saw his mother's maiden name on a tomb. When he read the inscription, his mouth dropped.

"Kevin Landry? Nawww… It can't be! Nawww… This is another Kevin Landry." He looked around again. "What year is this? I just saw my cousin. I just saw him!" He got on his knees in front of the tomb to get a closer look at the inscription.

Kevin Lyric Landry: February 17, 1985 - December 25, 2020

"That's today? How? I JUST saw him," he repeated to himself again and reached out to trace his fingers over the inscription. "Big cuz, what happened to you? And when? Because it can only be just after 2 in the morning…" he realized he didn't have his watch or phone to check the time.

Justice had been staring at the tomb so long, he didn't notice the woman standing next to him.

"Mama?" he said when he looked up at her. No response.

The woman wore a black veil and dress. He saw tears falling from underneath the veil and took note of the black and yellow roses in her hand. They were Kevin's favorite colors; his fraternity colors.

Justice's eyes went from the woman to the tomb several times before he knew she was not his mother. However, she was indeed the spitting image of her because she was Marilyn Landry, his auntie Lyn. His mother's identical twin sister.

In that moment, all the ignored phone calls, unreturned messages and calls, and missed visits to New Orleans to check on her weighed him down. He was guilt-heavy because he had no excuse for his neglect. When he turned eighteen, he ceased all communication with his aunt and thoughtlessly started sending large sums of money and elaborate gifts through the mail for her birthdays/Christmas and Mother's Day. For seventeen years, he avoided seeing her, but Justice knew she deserved the utmost respect. When his father passed two years after his mother, he was only twelve. With no hesitation, she shouldered the responsibility of both of his parents and raised him alongside Kevin. As he watched her mourn her son, Justice yearned to hug her and tell her he was sorry, he even tried, but his hands went through her. She couldn't see or hear him, so he stood by helplessly and listened for clues to what happened to his best friend.

"Why Kevin? Why would you take THAT plane? You always said that airline had quite a few issues in your opinion. It wasn't safe. You knew better baby! You knew better," she cried and leaned down to place the roses in front of the tomb.

"Plane? Kevin got on a plane after he left my condo? I thought he was leaving around 2 or 3 in the evening?" He thought about what Kevin said earlier. " Damn! That's right, he was low on cash, and the cheapest and earliest flight he could get out of Memphis was on… Spirit? No! No! No! Kevin knew better than that. We don't fly that shit!"

"Watch your mouth Justice! And yes, he flew Spirit."

He jumped at the sound of his mom's voice. She kept appearing out of nowhere.

"Ma! You gotta stop doing that!"

She continued. "Kevin's flight left at 3 AM… and I'm sorry baby, it went down in Lake Pontchartrain a few hours later. There were no survivors." Mrs. Benoit sadly delivered the details he had been waiting on.

"Kevin must've really been broke. I shoulda got him the plane ticket like he needed. No... I shoulda got US the plane tickets. I shoulda been on that later flight with him and helped pay for the party. I shoulda done more to help him with auntie Lyn. A lot more." The guilt was piling onto his shoulders. "Ma. Look at auntie Lyn.!" He pointed to his mother's grieving sister. He also realized he was no longer freezing. His mother's presence warmed him.

"Yeah. I know baby. But Kevin is fine. He's up in Heaven right now making the angels laugh. You know he's a comedian… always has been." She laughed, but Justice found nothing funny. "He's been there for about a week now. And you know I would do anything to bring him back to Lyn." She dropped her head in sorrow. "I just can't!"

Marilyn Landry stood by her son's tomb for a few more minutes, and then she walked away.

"Mama! You, Charity, and now Kevin? Don't you get it? All 3 of your deaths were because I dropped the ball. I get what you said about your passing, but there is nothing you can say to me to make me feel better about Charity and Kevin's death. Kevin was on THAT flight because he stayed behind to try to force me to do something I should have been excited to do on my own. If we would have left together right after Charity's event, we would've flown Delta or Southwest or something… anything better than Spirit. I just didn't want to go to auntie's party mama! I couldn't do it!"

"Justice, I hope you understand that Delta and Southwest planes sometimes go down too. So… you had nothing to do with the plane crashing baby. You must stop adding all that burden on yourself, it's too heavy for you to carry. And please tell me why you have treated my sister like an afterthought and a stranger all these years? I don't like that!"

Justice didn't know how to answer at first, but slowly came to the realization that honesty was the best response.

"Because of YOU mama! She looks just like you. Can you imagine how hard it was to look in her face every day after you died, and to know she's not you. She's Kevin's mama. Not mine. I just wanted mine!" He cried.

Mrs. Benoit's heart broke for her son. She didn't know what else to do, so she wrapped her arms around him and let him cry.

"Let it go Keys! Let it all go. Give it to mama!"

Justice leaned into his mother's chest and let go of twenty-five years of pain and regret. He cried so long, he drifted off to sleep... again.

JUSTICE K. BENOIT

It Came Upon A Midnight Clear
That glorious song of old

Justice was sleeping peacefully in his California king-sized bed when the sound of a piano playing woke him. He was no longer afraid of it because the tune was in the key of E flat, on the Alto clef.

"Mama!" He smiled.

Removing the covers from his body, he saw he was dressed in pajamas with a Christmas tree print.

"I know my mama did this to me," he said as he laughed. "She always put me in Christmas pajamas on Christmas Eve." He picked up his watch from the nightstand and looked at it.

"10:15 PM. December 24, 2020. Huh? How did I go back in time? And why 10:15 exactly?"

The piano playing stopped.

Justice needed answers and fast.

"The sunroom!" He jumped out of bed and ran to see if his mother was in there. The doors were closed. Nervously, he pushed them open and walked in. It was dark, and the piano was covered with the sheet.

Justice became aggravated with the emotional rollercoaster he had been on that night, and he finally broke.

"Aghhh! Aghhh!" he screamed. "I hate this! Mama this is crazy! Why did you show me all of this and leave me? What do I do now? I know what's about to happen today, so you're making me live through it AGAIN? WHY?" he punched the air and screamed louder.

The piano playing started again, and his mother's sweet voice filled the dark room.

"Justice, your dad and I talked about it, and we gave you something for Christmas you always thought you had in abundance. But we think you learned tonight that you didn't. Remember, your dad and I love you very much. Hurry, your gift is at the front door. We'll be watching. Goodbye son."

The piano playing stopped.

"Gift? Front door?" He was confused, but his mom told him to hurry, so he ran to his front room and arrived in time to witness "himself" letting Kevin in.

Knock... Knock... Knock...

"Kevin... cuz... I thought you was Charity. How you get up here? And why you ain't call first?" he asked as he swung the door open.

As Justice watched the interaction between "himself" and Kevin from earlier in the night... for the third time. He was trying to figure out what his parents gave him for Christmas. What was his "gift"?

"10:15! 10:15! Why 10:15?" He continued watching.

"I'm leaving... but if you don't show up tomorrow night, don't bother

calling me again. We ain't cousins no more after that, and I mean that shit. My mama deserves better than your selfish ass neglect," said Kevin.

Justice watched in confusion as Kevin rushed out of the condo upset.

"Ok. I know he's going to run into Charity in the hallway now. Come on ma! What's the point of doing this to me again!" he yelled into the air at his mom.

For the first time in twenty-three years, Justice heard a deep, intimidating voice that belonged to none other than, Paul Benoit; his dad.

"Boy! Yell at ya' mama again, and I'm gon' come down there myself."

"Dad? I'm sorry! I didn't mean to yell at ma, but this is too much. And I'm sorry for how mean and distant I was to you after mama died. I loved you, but I missed mama and…"

"Stop… I know alla that son. I love you too, and I missed your mama so much, I guess I died of a broken heart. The doctors just wanna call it a heart attack." He laughed. "But we're happy now, and we want the same for you. And son, that Giselle woman is a 'NO' for me. You chose her because you know she is NOT the one for you. You have been purposely sabotaging yourself my boy. You keep choosing women for the wrong reasons because IF you chose one for the right reasons, you would have had to change your nonchalant, stubborn behavior to keep her, and you don't want to do that. THAT'S why nothing goes right for you son. You've been standing in your own way! Now… stop standing there being ungrateful. Your gift is at the front door. It's slipping away! Look at the clock! GO NOW!"

Paul Benoit's voice faded away, and Justice looked at the clock.

"10:30! Slipping away… Clock… Oh shit! My gift is TIME! They gave me the time back, and I'm wasting it!"

Justice immediately came up with an idea to make the miraculous "gift" even better.

He grabbed his phone off the coffee table and called someone he hadn't spoken to in years, Cali Langley, his old music manager. She was glad to hear from him. He told her what he needed, and when she asked about a budget, he told her that money was not a problem. He wanted the best of everything. Justice had millions in the bank because he had not touched a dime of his money from when he played piano professionally. He even had a couple of solid gold bars he received from a Saudi Arabian prince. In other words, money was not an issue for Justice Benoit. When Cali heard the magic words: There was no budget. She gladly started making late-night calls.

"11:10!" He looked at the wall clock. "I gotta get to the hallway!"

Justice ran through the door into the hallway to witness the conversation between Kevin and Charity. Seconds later, he saw "himself" walking down the hallway with the bag of trash.

"Nope! I'll take it from here. If I let the old me handle this, he'll mess it all up… again!"

Instincts told him to step "into" "himself". The new Justice stood in front of the old one, and like magic, the two became one.

The new Justice took over and was so excited to get a chance to right his wrongs, he damn near skipped down the hall.

"Wassup y'all? Cuzzo! Don't be gettin' too cozy with my woman mane!" he joked.

Kevin and Charity cut their eyes from the strange-acting, happy, joking Justice, to each other.

"What the hell?" they said in unison.

"Your woman? Justice, I don't have time for your mind games tonight. It's late. I see you've been drinking or high off somethin' because you're trippin' right now. Here, take this box!"

Charity was even more upset about Justice trying to play with her while making plans to visit Giselle.

He knew why she was upset. He was in the hallway before the old him, so he overheard Kevin's slip of the lip about Giselle.

He was about to make things right with Charity, but he pulled Kevin to the side first.

"Cuzzo, lemme talk to you first. Charity, can you please hang out in my spot for a minute. I need to talk to Kev about my aunt."

Kevin and Charity's eyebrows shot up in surprise, and Charity agreed to let them talk in private. She left the box for Justice to bring in and walked to the door that was left open in the hallway.

"Kev, you're going to get a call from a New York area code in a few minutes. It will be Cali Langley, and I need you to give her all the information she needs."

"J.B. I think Charity is right. You must be high or somethin'. Remember, I ain't messin with you like that no more… unless you gon' be ready to get on the plane this afternoon." He stopped. "And hold up… where Cali come from? You ain't seen her in years. You said you were done with the music thing. Dude, you all over the place… as usual."

"Kevin, shut up and listen. No… I ain't gettin' on no plane, and you ain't either... no time soon."

Ring! Ringggg!

Kevin's phone rang, and like Justice said, it was from a New York area code. He looked at Justice like he was crazy because he didn't know what the woman could possibly want with him at eleven at night… on Christmas Eve.

"Answer the damn phone, fool. She'll tell you what's up. Lemme go talk to Charity. I got some apologizin' and beggin' to do." He didn't get far before he thought of the boy in the red sneakers.

"Hold up cuz. I'ma walk down with ya'. Let me run and get my ummm… "security guard" right quick though."

Kevin knew Justice was headed to get his pistol, so he shook his head and reluctantly answered Cali's call.

When Justice walked into his condo, Charity was out on the balcony breathing in the fresh air. He snuck up behind her, wrapped his arms around her tightly, and whispered in her ear.

"I'm not going to L.A. And I'm done with that whole situation. I deserve better than her, and you deserve better than me. But I hope… no… pray... that you see I am trying to change. I got a lot of things to fix in my life, and I can't do them without you."

Charity rolled her eyes and turned to face him.

"So, you need me to do something for you? As usual, I am your worker bee. Don't you get it? Don't you SEE? I am more than that! But, like I said… Justice is STILL blind." She pulled away from him and walked back into the condo.

He started to let her go because he was used to people leaving him.

"Nope. Not this time. I want more out of life. I want a wife and kids and that whole white picket fence deal. And I don't want it with just no anybody." He pushed away from the rail and went back in.

"Charity, stop!" He saw her walking out the door.

"What you need me to do? How can I prove I really SEE you? What? Tell me."

"I can't do that for you Justice. You have to figure that out on your own. I've done enough."

"Ok! Ok! Charity. I give up. We'll always be friends, and I guess I'll have to accept that. At least let me walk you down so I can get the other box of books and my caramel cake out your car."

"You give up?" she laughed. "You always say that AFTER you half-assed tried something. Some stuff you shouldn't give up on so easily." She shook her head. "But… Yeah… that's fine. You can walk me down. And… how did you know I had another box? And who said I brought yo' greedy butt a cake?"

"I just know. Shit… maybe I'm psychic or something!" He smirked. "But… hold up…" He ran to his bedroom to get his pistol and came right back. "I'm ready now. Come on. Let's go. And if you think you leaving this time of night to drive back home. You're wrong! It's too late for you to be out driving around Memphis. I would be less of a man if I let you do that baby girl. You can leave in the morning. I got some pajama pants for you to sleep in… or you can sleep naked if you like?"

Charity was glad he wasn't going to let her leave so late. She had planned to spend the night anyway, but she would definitely be sleeping in pajamas.

"Boy please! I ain't givin' you none. So, stop!"

"Hey… you can't blame a man for trying with yo' fine ass!"

Justice locked his door to walk Charity to her car, and Kevin ran up and bear-hugged him.

"Manneee… you're the best cousin ever! This shit gon' be epic!"

"Fool, get off me." Justice playfully shoved Kevin away and laughed because he knew why he was so excited. Truthfully, he was just as excited as he was. In a few hours, everything in his life was going to change… for the better.

He looked at his cellphone.

"12:00… on the dot." He patted his waistline for his "security guard", pushed the elevator button, and pulled Kevin and Charity in for a group hug as they stepped on the elevator.

Although she was in her feelings, she enjoyed the sentimental moment with her two longtime friends.

"Merry Christmas family!" he said to them, and then looked up to the ceiling.

"Happy Birthday mama. And thanks to you and dad for my Christmas gift. It was just what I needed… I just didn't know it. I love you both."

The elevator doors closed.

EPILOGUE

JUSTICE KEYS

Christmas Day 2020

"**M**erry Christmas and good evening Memphis. I was walking around the building earlier, and I must say… y'all look goodt… yes… goodt… with a 't' at the end!" The audience laughed. "I pray that everyone's holiday was everything they hoped it would be, and that you're ready for the EXTRAORDINARY finale. But first, let me find out what Santa brought some of y'all this morning. And if some of y'all were naughty and didn't get nothin', I got a few goodie bags from our sponsors you can win." Kevin announced and walked down the steps into the audience to play games and pass the time while everyone backstage was getting ready.

Backstage

"Everyone has arrived but the guest of honor. The Prevosts were supposed to be here at 8. It's 8:30. We gotta start soon. We only got the building until midnight." Cali stressed to Justice.

"Cali, chill. I got the text a few minutes ago. They're already in Memphis, and they just left the Westin headed here… and before you panic… it's right across the street remember?" He laughed at his manager's frustration because he was cool as a fan. Cali had done an amazing job of pulling a night to remember together.

"Mr. Benoit, go get dressed. I just got word that she's walking in now," Cali said, after talking to someone in her headset.

Forty-five of Justice and Kevin's family members had been bussed in from New Orleans on the finest tour buses money could rent. The crashing plane spooked Justice so bad, he didn't want anyone he loved on a plane regardless of the airline.

The New Orleans entourage entered the building and was awed by the Winter Wonderland in front of them. Justice had spared no expense when it came to Christmas decorations.

"What is going on? What y'all lookin' at? I been asking ever since we left New Orleans. And why I have to sit on that darn bus for 6 hours? I woulda got to Memphis much quicker on a plane. And why am I in Memphis anyway? Why I gotta wear this damn blindfold? Where y'all got me at? And where the hell is my son?" she was complaining and getting angrier by the minute.

One of the members of the family opened the door to her surprise, and they walked into the dimly lit room.

Kevin was still walking around entertaining the crowd when he saw his family walk in.

"It's Showtime!" he said to himself and turned the microphone off. He rushed down the aisle to meet them.

"I am going to ask one last time, then I am snatching this blindfold OFF! Where am I?" Marilyn Landry demanded.

"Mama? Why you down here being mean? It's Christmas,

stop being a Grinch!" Kevin joked and turned to his family. "What's up fam? Thanks for bringing my mama down that highway safely. Did she complain the entire ride?" All forty-five of his family members said, "YES!" and then laughed at each other.

"Kevin?" She finally removed the blindfold, and the first face she saw was her son's. "Boy you..." She halted the tongue-lashing she was about to give him when she noticed there were more people watching her than her family. Wayyy more. 15,000 to be exact.

Cali Langley booked the FedEx Forum for Justice early Christmas morning. She also booked transportation for his family to come from New Orleans, hotel rooms, caterers, decorators, secured sponsors, and spoke with realtors about a Christmas gift for another special woman in his life. Finally, he talked Kevin into dusting off his old comedic chops to host the event.

"Oh my God! This place is beautiful. Look at all the Christmas trees! They are gorgeous! Kevin, what's all of this?"

Without answering, Kevin turned the microphone on and motioned to one of the stage runners. Seconds later, smoke covered the stage, and the thick black curtains slowly opened.

"Ok everyone, remember what we talked about?" The audience yelled, "Yes!". "Ok. Good! This beautiful woman right here." Kevin hugged his mom. "Is the guest of honor. She is MY mother, and today is her 60th birthday... Don't she look good for her age? Y'all know black don't crack!" Everyone laughed. "So... all of this is for her."

"Whaaat?" Marilyn Landry said in shock and threw her hands over her mouth. "For me? But how did you pull all of this off?" She lowered her voice so no one would hear her.

"Kevin baby, you ain't got no money. You just borrowed $20 from me a few days ago. You're broke sweetie!"

The entire audience bursted into laughter because they heard her loud and clear. The microphone was ON and picked up what she thought was private.

"Ok! Ok! As you can see, my mama is the O.G. comedian in the family." He spoke into the mic and laughed, but he was beyond embarrassed.

Cali's voice came through the headphones he wore and gave him instructions.

Kevin pointed to the seats reserved for his family and helped his mom to her front row seat. After they were all seated, he pointed to the stage. A woman in a chef's hat rolled a three-tier cake on stage with the number 60 at the very top.

"Mama! This is another one of your surprises! Ok everyone. On the count of 3. 1… 2… 3…!" The audience sang:

Happy Birthday to you… Happy Birthday to you… Happy Birthday to…" The voices of the audience trailed off, and the cake was rolled to the back again. The next thing they heard was the melodious and distinctive voice of Stevie Wonder. When the curtains fully opened, he was sitting at a piano playing his soulful rendition of the birthday song.

"My God! Is that STEVIE on that stage?" Marilyn stood to her feet. "Sing Stevie!" she yelled at the stage as he flowed into a mini concert. Kevin had given him a list of her favorite Stevie Wonder songs. Starting with "Isn't She Lovely" and ending with "Overjoyed". Marilyn danced in her seat and up and down the front row with her other family members. She was having the time of her life.

When the concert was over, Kevin went back to his hosting duties.

"Alright everyone! Simmer down. We would like you to know that every dime from tonight's event will be donated to The Brain Aneurysm Foundation. Would the representatives from that organization come out here please?" Two men dressed in black suits walked onto the stage. A third person ran out to hand Kevin a huge check.

"Gentlemen, twenty-five years ago on Christmas Eve in this very building, my cousin; Justice, lost his mother, and my mother's twin sister to a brain aneurysm. Tonight, would've been her 60th birthday too." He paused to get his emotions together. His auntie Carolyn was his favorite aunt, and he missed her dearly. "That was a hit to our family that we've never been able to recover from. But… on that day, my mother vowed to give her time and money to bring awareness to brain research. So… this is a check for $100,000 on behalf of my mother; Marilyn Landry, to help in the fight against aneurysms and other brain-related illnesses." He looked at his mother. She was on her feet in tears mouthing the words: Thank you. She had been working day and night to get the word out about aneurysm symptoms. She didn't want anyone else to be in the dark about going to the doctor when symptoms arose.

She smiled because she figured out where all the money was coming from. Marilyn looked around but didn't see him.

The men left the stage with the check, and Kevin continued.

"Next on Santa's list… Charity Bingham? Where ya' at girl?" Kevin put a hand over his eyes to try to see the audience in the darkness. "Y'all we got an International Best-Selling Author in the house tonight. Where ya' at Charity B.?"

Reluctantly, she stood up from her front row seat. Her dad and sister; Grace, were seated next to her, and they forced her to do it. They had been in contact with Cali and Justice that day as well, so they knew what was about to happen.

"Spotlight please!" Kevin yelled.

Suddenly, a bright light shined over Charity's head, and she blushed from embarrassment. She didn't like that type of attention.

Several women she recognized from various domestic shelters

around the city walked up to her smiling. They all hugged her and thanked her for their Christmas gift.

"Aweeee ladies, I'm glad you enjoyed the pampering event and food this morning. And I really hope you enjoy my new book and the other goodies I put in your gift baskets." She dropped her head. "I wish I could do more than this annual event."

"More?" They said all at once. Then one spoke up.

"Charity, you gave us stability and peace of mind for Christmas. For women like us, that means everything. We can get on our feet and keep our kids safe now. What more could you want to do? That's the best Christmas gift on earth."

"Stability? Huh? What are y'all talking about?"

She was confused, so she cut her eyes to the stage. Kevin was walking down the steps. He stopped to hug his mom and headed straight towards her.

"Ms. Bingham, this is yours." He handed her a small box wrapped in beautiful black angel paper.

"Mine? Kevin, what is going on? What is this?" She opened the box with all 15,000 eyes watching her.

"Keys? What do these keys open, Kevin?" Charity was more confused than ever.

"Now. Take this too." He handed her an envelope.

"Kevin, who is this from?"

"Girl, read the papers." He laughed.

"Ohhh k! Let's see here… wait… these are the papers I saw at Justice's house last night. Where is he?" She looked around.

"Don't worry about where that busy-body boy is. Just read… I gotta get back to the stage, but Merry Christmas Charity." He hugged her and got back on the microphone to keep the crowd hype.

The spotlight was turned off, and the women from the shelter went back to their seats to enjoy the rest of the show. Charity sat down to open the envelope. Thumbing through the papers, she finally understood what she was looking at. "Archer Advertising agent: Justice Benoit Production Approval Contract. Bill Thacker Productions... Screenplay adaptation: *All is Fair in Love*... Author: Charity C. Bingham. TV series... OWN Network... Author/Writer signature: **Charity C. Bingham..**

Huh? Who signed this?" She flipped through a few more pages and found the deed to a building on Park Ave. It was in her name.

"I own this? How? Who did this? How did they know?"

"Ummm... sis, I kinda ummm... signed your name," Grace spoke up.

Charity looked over at her little sister and started sucking her teeth. She knew her sister had done something crazy.

"What you do Grace?"

"Welll... this morning when daddy and Justice were putting the gift baskets together. He asked daddy what you wanted for Christmas, and daddy called me, so I told him. Justice wanted to buy the building straight out and give it to you, but I know you wouldn't have accepted it. So... he told me about the TV series deal. He then made calls to push it through. Sis, the contract is very fair. Dad had his attorney look it over a few hours ago. You still own the rights to your characters and everything. You'll even get production credit. But anyway, it had to be done today because the building was a great price, but someone else already had a contract on it. Sis, it is everything you ever told me you wanted for a women's home, and it is in a safe location. Anyway, Justice threw his money and influence around, and the realtor was able to stop the other deal. He used cash as collateral and the TV production company backed it with a check in your name. After a little haggling over the price... you now have your first women's home sis, and the women here tonight have already been given apartments in the building."

Charity looked through the papers again.

"Grace! Y'all named it: The Faith Bingham House? In honor of mama. I love it. I love everything you did sis. Everything." She cried soft tears.

"I hate to say it C.C., but I didn't really do anything but sign your name. That was ALL Justice. But where did he get that type of money? I know that literary agency ain't payin' that much." Grace was curious about Justice's income, so Charity clued her in on what Justice told her about his childhood. Soon after, the lights went out in the building and everyone's attention was on the stage.

The curtains closed, and from the ceiling, a movie screen descended. The words: *Marilyn Landry: This Is Your Life* appeared on it.

Video footage and family pictures flashed slide after slide as the audience was wowed by Marilyn's childhood and life in New Orleans. Many cried when the footage of Hurricane Katrina and the Landry family on several Prevosts… again… appeared being bussed out of New Orleans hours before the levees broke.

Marilyn Landry sat on the front row crying at the memory of the flood. She also couldn't stop thinking about Justice because at the time, he was at Loyola University with Kevin, and without a second thought, he rented the buses and got every Landry and Benoit they could get in touch with out of the city.

"He is such a sweetheart. Just like his mama. He is just misunderstood. J.B. don't mean no harm really. I don't know why he is so distant from the family," Marilyn said to herself.

The images of her and Carolyn made her cry even harder because she missed her twin sister terribly. The final video was of Carolyn and Marilyn sitting in the front row of the FedEx Forum watching Justice's final performance as a professional piano player. Seeing her nephew's little body with his feet dangling from the piano bench made her sad. She missed him too.

"Where is Justice? He should be here? Where is my nephew?

I haven't seen him in years." She turned to one of her brothers. "Roy. This is crazy! J.B. just acts like we don't exist."

As Marilyn chatted with her brother, the video faded, and the screen ascended. Seconds later, the curtains opened again, and the stage was decorated in a breathtaking Christmas scene. In front of the scene were thirty members of the Lemoyne-Owen College Gospel Choir clad in beautiful purple and gold robes.

The floor opened, and a black baby grand piano rose from beneath the stage. When Marilyn, Roy, and everyone else in the Landry family saw the piano, their mouths dropped in awe. It was their family piano. The one their father and grandfather used to play on, and the same one that was housed in Carolyn's home for years and recently in the sunroom in Justice's condo.

Kevin walked from behind the stage and down the side steps to be by his mother's side. Microphone still in hand, he raised it to his mouth.

"Ladies and Gentlemen, this is the moment we've all been waiting for. Thirty-one years ago, a four-year-old piano prodigy born in New Orleans, LA and raised in Memphis, TN, wowed the world with his extraordinary ability to play by ear. His name was Justice Keys, and HE is my cousin." Kevin said proudly. "His innate talent granted him invitations to places most of us can only dream of visiting. He has played for Sultans in Afghanistan, 2 US Presidents; Clinton and Bush, and for the Queen of England along with many more, but something tragic happened on Christmas Eve in 1995 that stopped the music for our little prodigy... forever. As I mentioned earlier, his mother; my aunt Carolyn J. Landry-Benoit passed away that night, and my cousin's will to play left with her. He never touched the piano keys again. That is... until TONIGHT. For my mother's birthday, he will bless us with his first performance in 25 years. And it is all for you mama!" Kevin pointed to his mother. "So, without further ado... I present to you: Justice Keys Benoit!"

"Whaaat? Justice is here? He's going to play? For Me? Oh Kevin, that's the best gift ever. Thank you for getting him to play again!" Marilyn was jumping up and down in excitement.

"Yes. He is going to play just for YOU! And No ma. This was his idea. He decided on his own. As a matter of fact. Everything tonight was his doing. He wanted to make up for how he has been treating you for since his mama passed." He put his arm on her shoulder and told her to watch the stage.

Justice walked out slowly in his tailored tuxedo with the traditional tails and top hat like his mother used to love to see him in. He arrogantly did a spin in the middle of the stage and performed a hat trick where his top hat slid off his head and down his arm into his hand. He took the hat to the edge of the stage and motioned for Charity to come to him. She smiled and walked to him. He winked and handed her his top hat.

"Did you like your gift?" he asked.

"Yes, I did! It is amazing! Thank you."

"I guess I figured it out huh?"

"Yes. You did! You SEE me. You finally SEE me!"

"I do more than see you baby. I LOVE you!"

"Aweee! J.B. I love you too!"

Charity stood on her toes and met Justice halfway in a kiss. They remained lip-locked until Kevin got on the microphone and reminded him that he had a show to perform. The audience laughed.

He reluctantly pulled away from Charity and went back to his family's piano to take a seat. He put both hands on the keyboard and started playing with more passion than ever before. He was happy to play for his family and friends. As usual, he started with a medley of the classics... *Bach, Beethoven, Coltrane, etc.* and then allowed the choir to sing him into his grand finale.

Justice played with everything he had inside of him. He was

so into the euphoric feeling the sound of a piano gave him, he threw his head back and closed his eyes.

When he opened them, he saw his mom sitting on top of the piano enjoying her favorite song: ***It Came Upon A Midnight Clear.***

THE END.

**Merry Christmas
&
HAPPY NEW YEAR (2021)!**

AUTHOR BIO: CHINA

China was born and raised in Memphis, TN. She graduated from the University of Memphis with a bachelor's degree in Public Relations, and later received a master's degree in English Education from Union University. She released her first Urban Romance novel: *Tangled in a Lover's Web* (Co-authored with B'Shone), in the spring of 2019. A few months later, she released one of the two prequels to the story, *LACY: Caviar to Collard Greens*, and followed it up with *Tangled in a Lover's Web 2: Collapsed Web* (Co-authored with B'Shone), one year later. After the highly successful Tangled in a Lover's Web Series was released, China teamed up with her co-author again, and they flexed their writing skills to enter the world of Erotica. Months later, their collaboration produced the erotic mystery: *Sex in the Dark and Room 69: Freaky Tales*, a book of erotic short stories from the Hyde Park Ink Writing Squad feat. China. Proud of her accomplishments as an independent author, China took her writing skills to another level, and started an independent publishing and consulting company; Penhandler's Ink. Through her company, she motivates and shares her knowledge of content editing, character development, and plot execution, with burgeoning writers. As the Editor-in-Chief of Penhandler's Ink, China never hesitates to use her company's resources to help in her community. In the fall of 2020, she enlisted the help of five other independent authors to participate in a collaborative writing project; *SISTA WORLD: Twisted Tales.* The proceeds from this book will be donated to a charity that works to eradicate the existence of inequality in justice between men of color and women of color, regarding police brutality.

When China is not working to affect change in the world, she is training future authors and developing young minds in her role as a high school English teacher in Atlanta, GA. On the weekends, and during the summer months, she enjoys spending time with her daughter and granddaughter in Nashville, TN.